CORRECTIVE MEASURES

CORRECTIVE MEASURES

STORY
GRANT CHASTAIN

PENCILS
FRAN MOYANO

COLORS
JAY MOYANO

LETTERS
MIKE STORNIOLO
BRANT W. FOWLER

GRAPHIC DESIGN
DMF COMICS

owner/editor	art director	editor	editor	editor
Sean O'Reilly	**Todd Demong**	**Stjepan Sejic**	**Stefani Rennee**	**Kevin Hanna**

ARCANA STUDIO PRESENTS GRUNTS. First Printing.

Published by Arcana Comics, Inc. 11400 West Olympic Blvd, 14th Floor, Los Angeles, CA 90064, USA.

ISBN: 978-1-897548-22-6

Printed in Canada

CHAPTER 1

CORRECTIVE
MEASURES
J. BRODY

OCT. 6TH, 2007.
THERE IS AN ISLAND APPROXIMATELY 30 MILES OFF THE COAST OF FLORIDA. ATLANTIC SIDE.
THP THP THP THP

ONCE, IT WAS THE HOME OF A SECRET MILITARY INSTALLATION.
THP THP THP THP THP THP
TODAY... IT'S A PRISON.

A PLACE FOR SUPER-POWERED SCUMBAGS AND THEIR KEEPERS.
GOD TESTED DANIEL BY SENDING HIM INTO THE LION'S DEN... SO, TOO, IS HE TESTING ME.

BY CASTING MY SOUL INTO THE VERY MOUTH OF EVIL.

GET THE FUCK OUT!

WELCOME TO SAN TIBURON, SIR.
YOU ARE TO LIE DOWN ON THE TARMAC UNTIL WE CAN FIT YOU WITH A RESTRAINING NECKLACE.
IF THE GUARDS DETECT ANY SUDDEN MOVEMENT FROM YOU, THEY WILL OPEN FIRE.
ARE MY DIRECTIONS CLEAR?
THY KINGDOM COME...
HEY--ASSHOLE! I ASKED YOU IF MY INSTRUCTIONS WERE CLEAR!
WHAT ARE YOU, DEA--
...THY WILL BE DONE.
AGGHHH!
WHAMMMM
BAMM
BAMMM
MMMFFFF!

THEY DON'T GET IT YET. BUT THEY WILL.
I'M NOT LOCKED IN HERE WITH THEM.
FUCK...
BROKE MY FUCKIN' NOSE!
PFFTTT
THEY'RE LOCKED IN HERE WITH ME.
SITUATION UNDER CONTROL. WE'VE GOT HIM, CENTRAL COMMAND.
I REPEAT - WE'VE GOT...
CROSSED OUT
STORY * PENCILS * COLORS * LETTERS
Grant Chastain Fran Moyano Jay Moyano Mike Storniolo

PAYBACK. IN THE FLESH.
YOU'RE KIDDING ME.
GOD'S WITNESS.
YOU SHOULD HAVE BEEN UP ON THE PLATFORM.
HE REARRANGED DWIGHT'S FACE WITHOUT BREAKING A SWEAT.
IT WAS HILARIOU
Warden Devlin
ANYWAY, GOT AN INTERVIEW WITH DEVLIN AT TEN FOR THE OPEN CAPTAIN'S SLOT.
A PAY INCREASE, PLUS THE CHANCE TO WATCH A COUPLE THESE EVIL SONS-A-BITCHES KILL EACH OTHER EVERY SO OFTEN?
I DON'T EVEN NEED A DENTAL PLAN... JUST SIGN ME UP!
HA-HA!
THAT'S GOOD TO KNOW, OFFICER...
I'LL BE SURE TO MENTION YOUR SENTIMENTS TO WARDEN DEVLIN WHEN I SPEAK WITH HIM.
I THINK WE CAN CONSIDER YOUR INTERVIEW CONCLUDED, DO YOU AGREE?
Y-YES SIR, ASSISTANT WARDEN.
SPLENDID. PERHAPS YOU'D BEST BE RETURNING TO YOUR POST, BEFORE I ENTERTAIN YOUR REQUEST FOR IMMEDIATE REVOCATION OF YOUR DENTAL INSURANCE.
Warden Devlin

KNOCKIN' BEFORE ENTERING... WE'RE NOT DOING THAT ANYMORE?
YOUR TEN A.M. INTERVIEW ACCEPTED A BETTER OFFER.
JUST THOUGHT YOU'D CARE TO KNOW THAT WALTER ANTHONY LOCKE WAS PROCESSED AND ADMITTED THIS MORNING.
AHH, YES. "PAYBACK". I REMEMBAH WHEN THE COSTUMES USED TO TAKE PRIDE IN SELECTING A NAME.
NOW IT'S ALL "WAR" THIS AND "BLOOD" THAT. NO SUBTLETY ANYMORE.
HE A HARD ASS?
HE'LL BREAK.
DON'T THEY ALL.
YOU KNOW, WE'RE STILL SHORT-HANDED IN VIOLENT CRIME.
FUNNY... YOU KEEP CANCELLIN' MY INTERVIEWS.

I JUST SPOKE TO HARVEY AT STATEVILLE. THEY'VE GOT A GUY UP THERE I'D LIKE TO BRING DOWN FOR A TEST-DRIVE.
JASON BRO
FORMER MILITARY, REAL GO-GETTER.
I'LL BE FLYING UP THIS AFTERNOON, SO YOU'LL BE FOR A LITTLE WHILE. DON'T THROW ANY WILD PARTIES WHILE I'M GONE.
A LOT OF GUYS HERE WERE WAITING ON THAT JOB, SIR. AN OUTSIDE HIRE WON'T BE A POPULAR DECISION. I DON'T THINK--
AND I DON'T THINK I NEED YOU TO TELL ME HOW TO RUN MY PRISON. ASSISTANT WARDEN.
NOW...DO. WE. HAVE. A. PROBLEM?
NO SIR.
I THOUGHT NOT.
YOU CAN GO NOW. IF YOU NEED ME...

JOG DOWN THIS OR THAT SIDEWALK.

TAKE THIS OR THAT ROAD.

AND YET, THE ***CHOICES*** WE ALLOW OURSELVES TO MAKE GIVE US THE ***ILLUSION*** OF FREE WILL.

IT IS A DEFENSE MECHANISM. TOO MANY OPTIONS, AND YOUR LIFE FEELS UNMANAGEABLE. TOO FEW AND YOU FEEL SUFFOCATED.

INCARCERATED.

SPLINTERS.
THE FINELY-TUNED SHARPNESS OF OUR MEMORIES...
...TINY SHARDS OF MY LIFE, PASSING BEFORE ME...
...AS I FLOAT ON A CLOUD ABOVE THE FRAY...
...MY LIFE... AILEEN... MEGHAN, OUR BABY...
...I'LL NEVER SEE THEM AGAIN, UNLESS I CAN WAKE UP... WAKE UP...
WAKE UP.

WELCOME TO WING FOUR AT STATEVILLE CORRECTIONAL CENTER.
TODAY, WE'RE EXPERIENCING WHAT I LIKE TO CALL A "MINOR DISTURBANCE."
AS THE ON-DUTY CAPTAIN HERE AT WING FOUR, YOU'D PROBABLY EXPECT ME TO KNOW *WHY* THIS IS HAPPENING.
SECURITY
SECURITY
TRUTH BE TOLD... I HAVEN'T A CLUE.
DRUG WAR. GANG DISPUTE. SOMEBODY WANTED AN EXTRA HELPING OF MASHED POTATOES.
SOMEBODY SMUDGED SOMEONE ELSE'S TENNIS SHOE.
THERE'S ALWAYS *SOME* REASON TO BLOW UP THE SPOT.
I CAN'T CONCERN MYSELF WITH THE WHY.
THIS HAS TO END. *NOW.*
SECURITY

JEFFERSON!
ENOUGH!
MOTHERFU--
WHOOOF
UNGGHH!
WHOOOMPH!
YOU'RE **DEAD**, BOSS!
I'M 'MA **KILL** YO' ASS! YOU HEAR ME? I'M 'MA KIL--
RAHRRR!

STEP OVER THIS OR THAT WOUNDED OFFICER.
ATTACK THIS OR THAT INSTIGATOR.
SLSSHHH
USE THIS OR THAT AVAILABLE SHARD OF GLASS TO PUNCTURE THIS OR THAT LUNG.
IN PRISON AND LIFE... YOU PAY FOR YOUR CHOICES IN BLOOD.
EVEN IF IT'S NOT YOUR OWN.
SECURITY
SECURITY
SECURITY

I CAN'T BELIEVE WHAT I'M HEARING.
WARDEN MCMULLAN
CAPTAIN, THE MAN'S FAMILY IS FILING SUIT AGAINST THE STATE OF ILLINOIS, THE BUREAU OF PRISONS, AND THE UNITED STATES GOVERNMENT FOR USE OF EXCESSIVE FORCE.
YOU PUT US IN A DIFFICULT POSITION HERE.
SECURITY
DON'T KID YOURSELF. THIS IS NOTHING MORE THAN A BIG GAME OF C.Y.A.
AND DON'T THINK I DON'T KNOW WHOSE "A" YOU'RE COVERING.
EFFECTIVE IMMEDIATELY, YOU ARE HEREBY RELIEVED OF YOUR COMMAND.
AFTER ONE WEEK OF PAID LEAVE COMMENSURATE WITH YOUR INJURY, YOU WILL BE PUT IN AN UNPAID ADMINISTRATIVE LEAVE PENDING A HEARING.
DO YOU UNDERSTAND THESE TERMS?
YOU'RE NOT GOING TO GET AWAY WITH THIS.
CAPTAIN
OFFICERS, PLEASE COLLECT MISTER BRODY'S KEYS AND BADGE, AND ESCORT HIM TO THE PARKING LOT.
IF HE RETURNS, OR CAUSES A DISTURBANCE ON HIS WAY OUT... ARREST HIM.

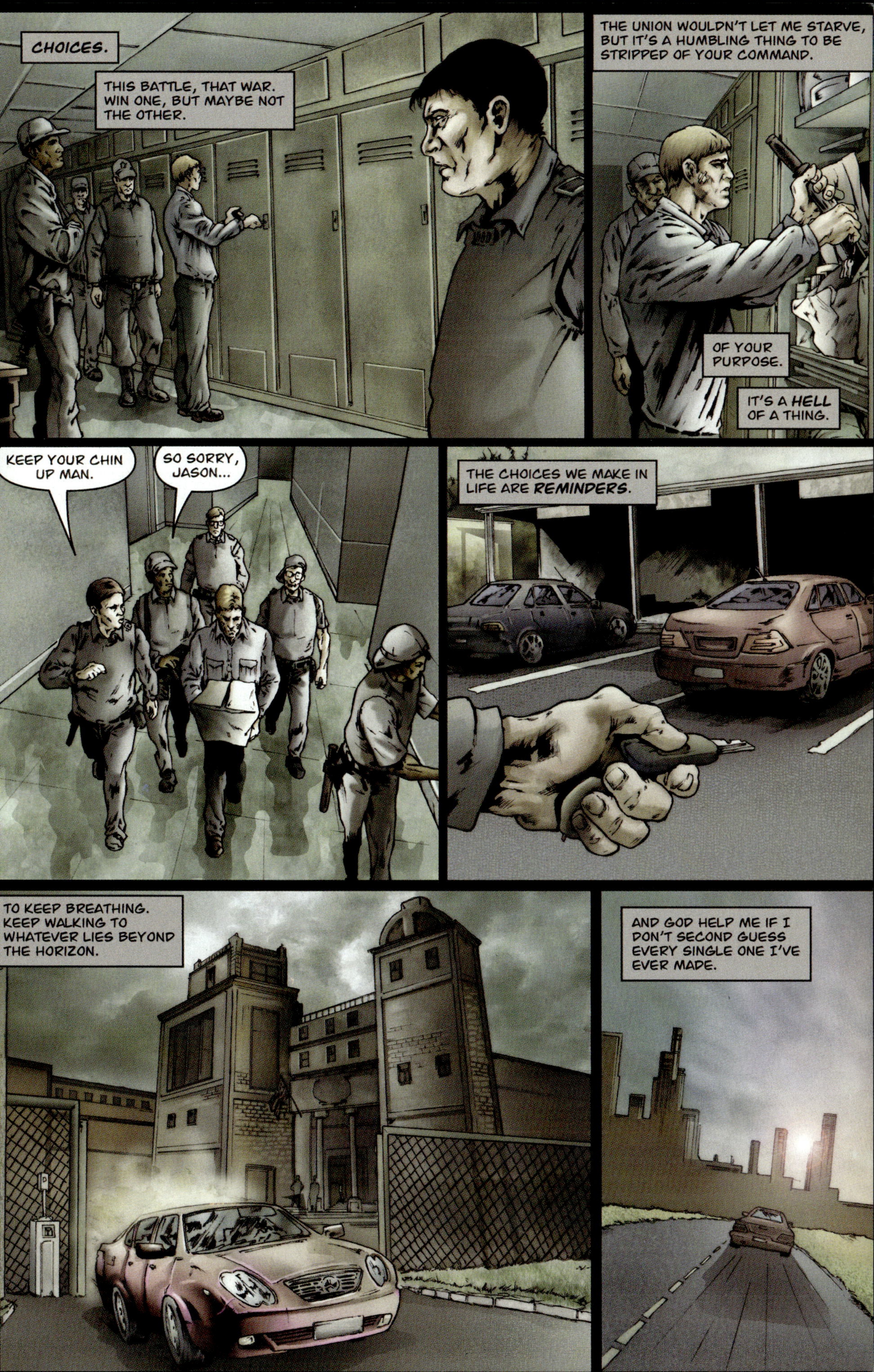

CHOICES.

THIS BATTLE, THAT WAR. WIN ONE, BUT MAYBE NOT THE OTHER.

THE UNION WOULDN'T LET ME STARVE, BUT IT'S A HUMBLING THING TO BE STRIPPED OF YOUR COMMAND.

OF YOUR PURPOSE.

IT'S A **HELL** OF A THING.

KEEP YOUR CHIN UP MAN.

SO SORRY, JASON...

THE CHOICES WE MAKE IN LIFE ARE **REMINDERS**.

NICE LITTLE HOME YOU'VE GOT HERE.
BET THOSE PROPERTY TAXES ARE A REAL BITCH, THOUGH.
HOUSE ON A CORNER LOT LIKE THIS.
CAN I HELP YOU WITH SOMETHING?
ACTUALLY, SON... I'M HOPING WE CAN HELP **EACH OTHER.**
YOU MIND IF I STEP INSIDE? HUMIDITY THIS TIME OF YEAR IS HELL ON MY LUNGS.
MISTER, I DON'T WANT TO BE RUDE... BUT I REALLY HAVE TO GO AND I REALLY DON'T WANT ANY OF WHAT YOU'RE SELLING.
SO IF YOU DON'T MIND...
THE NAME'S CLARKE DEVLIN. AND TRUST ME SON...
YOU **WANT** WHAT **I'M** SELLIN'.
DEVLIN
CLARKE
United States

WARDEN DEVLIN PROCEEDED TO TELL US A STORY.
ABOUT A PLACE CALLED SAN TIBURON. AND THE KIND OF CRIMINALS THEY KEEP THERE.
IT'S EASY TO FORGET ABOUT THEM --
AFTER THE TRIAL, WHEN THE CAPES AND COSTUMES AND NEWSPAPERS HAVE MOVED ON TO OTHER MENACES.
AFTER THE CAMERAS HAVE ALL STOPPED FLASHING. WHEN EVERYBODY ELSE HAS GONE HOME TO THEIR FAMILIES - THEY DON'T GO HOME.
THEY GO TO SAN TIBURON.
WARDEN DEVLIN SAID THEY HAVEN'T HAD A SINGLE ESCAPED PRISONER IN THE 27 YEARS SINCE THE PRISON OPENED. NOT ONE.
IT ALL SEEMED TOO GOOD TOO BE TRUE. HOW COULD A PLACE LIKE THAT WORK?
PERSONNEL FILE
CLASSIFIED
AND HE SHOWED ME.
ASK SON, AND YE SHALL RECEIVE.
PERSONNEL FILE

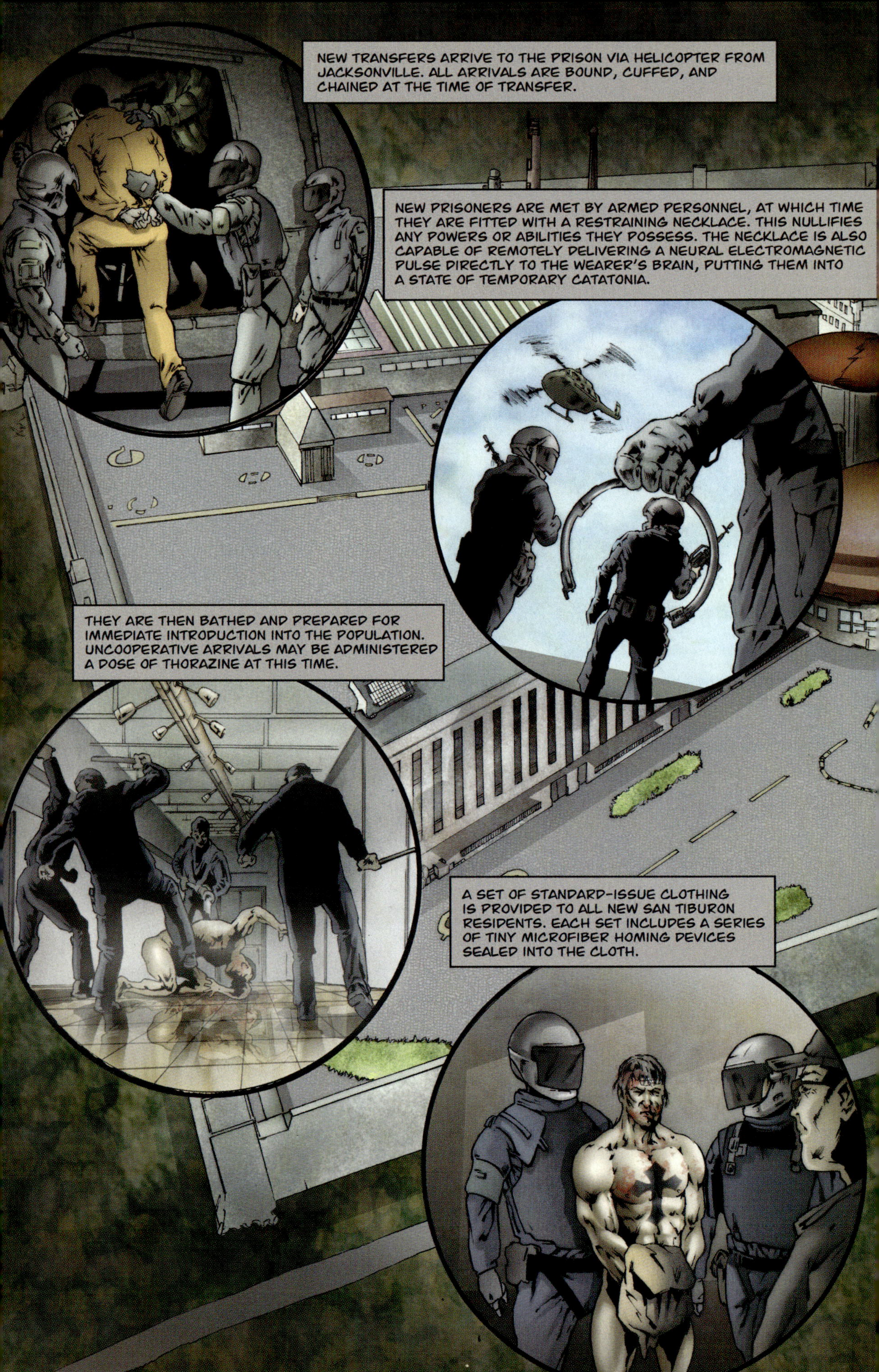
NEW TRANSFERS ARRIVE TO THE PRISON VIA HELICOPTER FROM JACKSONVILLE. ALL ARRIVALS ARE BOUND, CUFFED, AND CHAINED AT THE TIME OF TRANSFER.
NEW PRISONERS ARE MET BY ARMED PERSONNEL, AT WHICH TIME THEY ARE FITTED WITH A RESTRAINING NECKLACE. THIS NULLIFIES ANY POWERS OR ABILITIES THEY POSSESS. THE NECKLACE IS ALSO CAPABLE OF REMOTELY DELIVERING A NEURAL ELECTROMAGNETIC PULSE DIRECTLY TO THE WEARER'S BRAIN, PUTTING THEM INTO A STATE OF TEMPORARY CATATONIA.
THEY ARE THEN BATHED AND PREPARED FOR IMMEDIATE INTRODUCTION INTO THE POPULATION. UNCOOPERATIVE ARRIVALS MAY BE ADMINISTERED A DOSE OF THORAZINE AT THIS TIME.
A SET OF STANDARD-ISSUE CLOTHING IS PROVIDED TO ALL NEW SAN TIBURON RESIDENTS. EACH SET INCLUDES A SERIES OF TINY MICROFIBER HOMING DEVICES SEALED INTO THE CLOTH.

EACH POD IS ENCASED IN TWELVE INCHES OF SOLID TITANIUM, AND LOCKED BEHIND A CLEAR, IMPENETRABLE DOOR. VOICE AUTHORIZATION IS REQUIRED TO OPEN A LOCKED POD.
WING ASSIGNMENT IS PREDETERMINED. THERE ARE FOUR WINGS - VIOLENT CRIME, NON-VIOLENT CRIME, SEXUAL CRIME, AND THE PSYCHIATRIC WARD.
THE NEW ARRIVAL IS SLOWLY INTEGRATED INTO THE GENERAL POPULATION OVER THE COURSE OF A WEEK, TO ENSURE MAXIMUM SAFETY FOR ALL.
IN THE MEANTIME, WE ENCOURAGE ALL NEW RESIDENTS TO SPEND AS MUCH TIME AS POSSIBLE GETTING USED TO THEIR NEW SURROUNDINGS.

I DIHN'T COME HERE FOR YOUR **COFFEE**, MISTER BRODY. I CAME HERE TO OFFAH YOU A JOB.
I NEED A CAPTAIN FOR MY VIOLENT CRIME WING, AND AS OF TODAY, YOU'RE OFFICIALLY AN **UNSIGNED FREE AGENT**.
MISTER DEVLIN, I APPRECIATE THE... UH, **VERY** KIND OFFER, BUT... I'M NOT EVEN SURE IT'S **LEGAL** CONSIDERING THE CHARGES AGAINST ME.
THOSE CHARGES DISAPPEARED THE MINUTE I OFFERED YOU THE JOB.
WAYS AND MEANS, SON.
MISTER DEVLIN, THIS IS ALL HAPPENING PRETTY QUICKLY. I NEED SOME TIME TO THINK IT ALL OVER.
MY BUSINESS CARD, MISTER BRODY. I'LL BE OUTSIDE IN YOUR DRIVEWAY TOMORROW MORNING, AT EIGHT... 'LESS YOU CALL THAT NUMBER AND TELL ME TO **FUCK OFF**.
EXPECT YOU WON'T BE LATE.

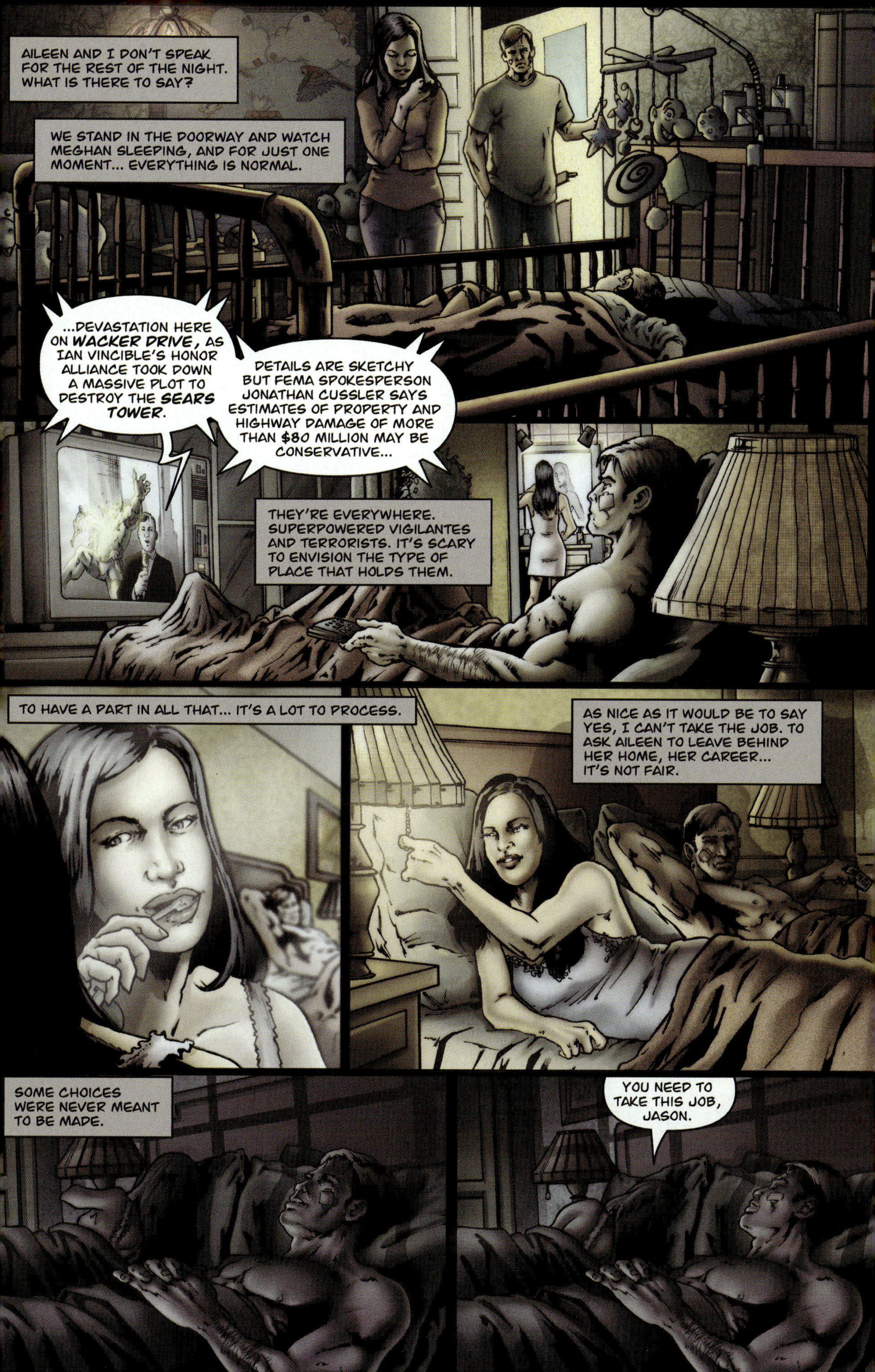
AILEEN AND I DON'T SPEAK FOR THE REST OF THE NIGHT. WHAT IS THERE TO SAY?
WE STAND IN THE DOORWAY AND WATCH MEGHAN SLEEPING, AND FOR JUST ONE MOMENT... EVERYTHING IS NORMAL.
...DEVASTATION HERE ON WACKER DRIVE, AS IAN VINCIBLE'S HONOR ALLIANCE TOOK DOWN A MASSIVE PLOT TO DESTROY THE SEARS TOWER.
DETAILS ARE SKETCHY BUT FEMA SPOKESPERSON JONATHAN CUSSLER SAYS ESTIMATES OF PROPERTY AND HIGHWAY DAMAGE OF MORE THAN $80 MILLION MAY BE CONSERVATIVE...
THEY'RE EVERYWHERE. SUPERPOWERED VIGILANTES AND TERRORISTS. IT'S SCARY TO ENVISION THE TYPE OF PLACE THAT HOLDS THEM.
TO HAVE A PART IN ALL THAT... IT'S A LOT TO PROCESS.
AS NICE AS IT WOULD BE TO SAY YES, I CAN'T TAKE THE JOB. TO ASK AILEEN TO LEAVE BEHIND HER HOME, HER CAREER... IT'S NOT FAIR.
SOME CHOICES WERE NEVER MEANT TO BE MADE.
YOU NEED TO TAKE THIS JOB, JASON.

WHAT?
DON'T ACT LIKE I DON'T KNOW YOU, JASON.
YOU ALREADY KNOW THIS IS WHAT YOU WANT.
NO. THAT'S NOT FAIR TO YOU, YOUR JOB...
I'LL FIND ANOTHER JOB. THIS ISN'T ABOUT WHAT I NEED. YOU NEED THIS.
I DON'T HAVE TO TELL YOU IT'LL BE MORE DANGEROUS.
I KNOW.
ARE YOU OKAY WITH THAT?
NO. BUT WITH TIME, AND GENEROUS GIFTS OF JEWELRY, I'LL GET OVER IT.
JEWELRY, EH? ANYTHING ELSE?
CHOCOLATE.
AND FOOT RUBS.
I LOVE YOU, AILEEN...
I LOVE YOU TOO...
NOW KISS ME, YOU SILLY OLD BEAR, BEFORE I CHANGE MY MIND.

SO WHAT DO YOU SAY, SON? DO WE HAVE A DEAL?
CHOICES.
I'M IN, WARDEN. BUT I NEED TO SEE IT UP CLOSE BEFORE I MAKE MY FINAL DECISION.
I'D ALSO LIKE TO WORK WITH YOU TO MAKE SURE AILEEN FINDS EMPLOY-MENT. YOU SAID SOMETHING ABOUT CONNECTIONS WITH HOSPITALS?
DONE AND DONE, JASON.
I'M LOOKING FORWARD TO WORKING WITH YOU AS WELL, MRS. BRODY.
PLEASE, CALL ME AILEEN.
JUST BRING HIM BACK IN ONE PIECE, MISTER DEVLIN.
I'LL CALL YOU TONIGHT.
THE CHOICES WE MAKE HAVE THE POWER TO RESONATE. TO CHANGE US.
IF WE'RE LUCKY... WE MAY EVEN FIND SOMETHING IMPORTANT TO US. SOMETHING WE DIDN'T KNOW WE NEEDED.

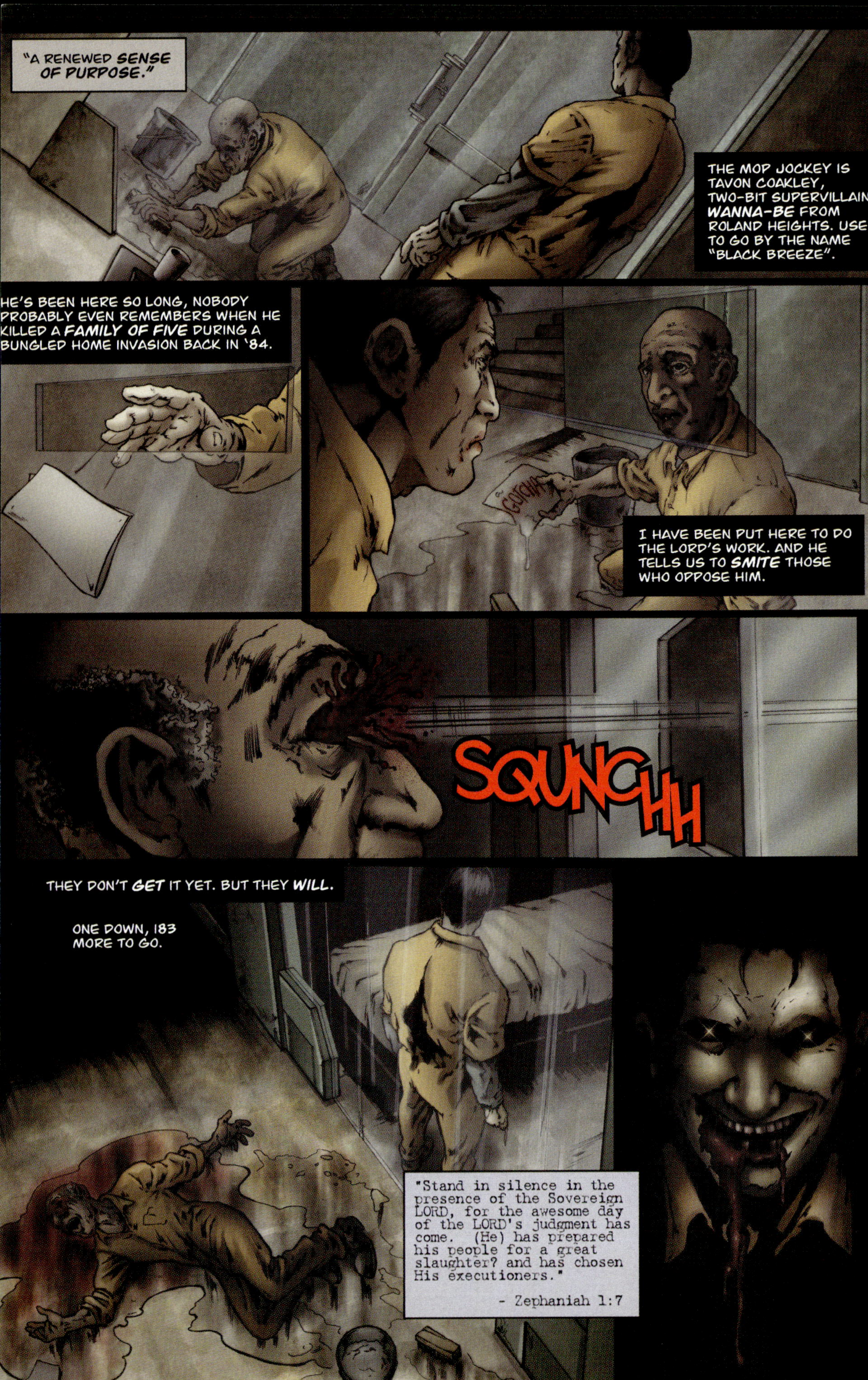

"A RENEWED **SENSE** OF PURPOSE."
THE MOP JOCKEY IS TAVON COAKLEY, TWO-BIT SUPERVILLAIN ***WANNA-BE*** FROM ROLAND HEIGHTS. USE TO GO BY THE NAME "BLACK BREEZE".
HE'S BEEN HERE SO LONG, NOBODY PROBABLY EVEN REMEMBERS WHEN HE KILLED A ***FAMILY OF FIVE*** DURING A BUNGLED HOME INVASION BACK IN '84.
I HAVE BEEN PUT HERE TO DO THE LORD'S WORK. AND HE TELLS US TO ***SMITE*** THOSE WHO OPPOSE HIM.
SQUNCHH
THEY DON'T ***GET*** IT YET. BUT THEY ***WILL***.
ONE DOWN, 183 MORE TO GO.
"Stand in silence in the presence of the Sovereign LORD, for the awesome day of the LORD's judgment has come. (He) has prepared his people for a great slaughter? and has chosen His executioners."
- Zephaniah 1:7

CHAPTER 2

CORRECTIVE
MEASURES
FRAN MOYANO 07

IT'S A THREE HOUR FLIGHT FROM CHICAGO O'HARE TO JACKSONVILLE.
FROM THE AIRPORT, WE'LL TAKE A SHUTTLE TO THE HARBOR. A FERRY WILL TAKE US TO THE ISLAND. ABOUT AN HOUR'S RIDE EACH WAY.
TO SAY THE LEAST...
IT'S A LONG COMMUTE.
LET'S HOPE THIS TRIP IS WORTH THE DISTANCE.
...BECAUSE I'M A LONG WAY FROM HOME.

SAN TIBURON IS A MAXIMUM SECURITY PENITENTIARY THAT OPERATES AS A CATCH-ALL FOR ANY PRISONER ARRESTED FOR METACRIMES.
THE MAJORITY OF THE PRISONERS INTERRED ARE ELIGIBLE FOR PAROLE... BUT THAT'S LIKE SAYING I'M ELIGIBLE TO PLAY FOR THE CHICAGO BULLS.
ONLY TWO PRISONERS WERE EVER PAROLED FROM THE FACILITY. ONE DIED IN A BANK HEIST... AND ONE WAS BACK INSIDE SAN TIBURON IN LESS THAN A YEAR.
HERE YOU GO, JASON...
...LITTLE LIGHT READIN' FOR THE LONG TRIP.
CONFIDENTIAL

AMAZING.

STATEVILLE WOULD OCCASIONALLY RECEIVE A NOTORIOUS CRIMINAL. SOME ACTOR OR CELEBRITY THAT WOUND UP ON THE WRONG SIDE OF A FENCE.

WE WATCHED HIS TRIAL ON TELEVISION FOR OVER A YEAR. THE CHRISTIAN SOLDIER WAGING HOLY WAR ON THOSE THAT WOULD DEFY THE WAYS OF THE LORD.
HE CALLED HIMSELF PAYBACK... BUT TO CRIMINALS, HE MAY AS WELL HAVE BEEN THE ANGEL OF DEATH.
IN SEPTEMBER 2007, WALTER ANTHONY LOCKE WAS CONVICTED OF 85 COUNTS OF FIRST-DEGREE MURDER... THOUGH THE PROSECUTORS ADMITTED WE MIGHT NEVER KNOW EXACTLY HOW MANY MEN AND WOMEN HE KILLED.
SECURITY FOOTAGE, 32ND AND 5TH. EXHIBIT C.
HE SMILED WHEN THEY SENTENCED HIM TO LIFE IMPRISONMENT.
PROBABLY BECAUSE HE KNEW WHERE HE'D BE GOING.

DOING OKAY OVER HERE?
THANKS FOR THE FILES, WARDEN. IT USUALLY HELPS TO KNOW WHO THE PROBLEM KIDS ARE BEFORE YOU ARRIVE.
NO QUESTION. ESPECIALLY THAT ONE THERE. HE'S PART OF THE REASON I BROUGHT YOU HERE.
I NEED SOMEONE TO HELP ME KEEP HIS ASS IN LINE.
IF IT'S ALL THE SAME I'D LIKE TO MEET WITH HIM ONE-ON-ONE.
I'VE FOUND THAT GUYS LIKE LOCKE RESPOND BETTER TO DIRECT MESSAGES.
HEY, IT'S YOUR UNIT... DO WHAT YOU THINK'S BEST.
THERE SHE IS.
TAKE A MOMENT. LET IT SINK IN.
WOW...
...YOU NEVAH FORGET YOUR FIRST TIME.

VIRTUE

STORY * PENCILS * COLORS * LETTERS

Grant Chastain* * *Fran Moyano* * *Jay Moyano* * *Mike Storniolo

MAINTENANCE IS WORKING ON THE SKY GONDOLAS, SO WE'RE GOING TO HAVE TO BUS YOU BOTH UP THE GATES, WARDEN. HOPE THAT'S OKAY.
FINE, JOHNNY, JUST FINE.
IF YOU COULD STEP THIS WAY, WE'LL BE MOVING OUT.
IT'S ABOUT A FOUR MILE DRIVE UP THE JUNGLE ROAD TO THE TOP-SHOULD TAKE ABOUT 25 MINUTES.
IS THIS... ER, SAFE?
SAFE? NOT P'TICULARLY. BUT HELL, DON'T LET *THAT* BOTHER YA...
"...ROUND HERE, THE TERM *SAFE* IS PRETTY *SUBJECTIVE.*"

GOD DAMN IT, JIMMY... FUCKIN' TRIP-QUEENS. THAT'S MY LAST CIGARETTE.
HEY, MAYBE YOU CAN GET A LOAN FROM LOCKE OVER THERE.
WAY HE'S STARING US DOWN, I'D SAY HE'S HUNGRY FOR YOUR HOLE.
ALRIGHT, I'D HAD ENOUGH OF THIS HORSE-SHIT...
GET FUCKED, FARACI.
YOU GOT SOMETHING YOU WANT TO SAY TO ME?
FUCK'S SAKE, JIMMY, COOL IT. THAT'S PAYBACK.
YOUR BROTHER BEGGED FOR HIS LIFE WHEN I CUT HIM OPEN.
WHAT'D YOU JUST SAY TO ME?
JIM!
JIMMY, LEAVE IT ALONE...
FUCK YOU, PSYCHO! I ASKED WHAT YOU SAID!
YOUR HEROIN-WORSHIPING SHIT OF A BROTHER BEGGED FOR HIS LIFE WHEN I CUT HIM OPEN, DIAMOND JIM.
HE BROKE THE FIRST COMMANDMENT. HOW MANY HAVE YOU BROKEN?

YOU MOTHER-FUCKER! I'LL RIP OFF YOUR HEAD!
LET ME GO, DICKY!
SITUATION?
GALLENTINI, SIR. ONE SECOND HE'S PLAYING CARDS, THE NEXT HE'S THROWING HIMSELF AT PAYBA... AT LOCKE, SIR.
HAVE COMMUNICATIONS ROLL BACK THE TAPE LATER. I WANT TO KNOW EXACTLY WHAT HE SAID. IN THE MEANTIME, END THIS SHIT.
BLEEP BLEEP BLOOP
ARRGHHHGHH!
I'LL SPEAK SLOWLY SO THERE WON'T BE ANY MIS-UNDERSTANDIN'.
THOSE NECKLACES Y'ALL ARE WEARIN' AIN'T FOR LOOKS.
IF YOU GET OUT OF LINE, YOU GET TO WEAR RUBBER DIAPERS IN SOLITARY LIKE JIMBO HERE.
QUESTIONS?
GOOD. HERE ENDETH THE LESSON.
OFFICERS, PLEASE TAKE THESE OTHER GENTLEMEN BACK TO THEIR PODS.
LEAVE MR. LOCKE BEHIND. HE'S GOT HISSELF A VISITOR THIS EVENIN'.

MR. LOCKE, I'D LIKE TO INTRODUCE YOU TO JASON BRODY. BRODY'S GOING TO BE THE NEW CAPTAIN OF VIOLENT CRIME, SO HE'S GONNA BE YOUR NEW POPPA.
THAT **ALRIGHT** BY YOU, WALTER?
WELL, HOO-RAY IF'N IT IS, AND **FUCK YOU** IF'N IT AIN'T.
THANKS, WARDEN.
TAKE AS MUCH TIME AS YOU NEED WITH THIS ONE, CAPTAIN. THESE GUYS'LL SHOW YOU TO THE **DUTY OFFICE** AFTER YOUR DONE.
CLICK

YOU'RE PROBABLY WONDERING WHY I WANTED TO SPEAK WITH YOU.
SEE, I GET WHY EVERYBODY ELSE IS IN HERE, THEY'RE ALL LYING CRIMINAL SHITBAGS.
BUT YOU... YOU'RE DIFFERENT. WANT TO TELL ME WHY YOU ENDED UP IN HERE?
RIGHT... WELL, THEN I GUESS YOU WON'T MIND IF I SIT HERE FOR AWHILE. I'VE GOT LOTS OF TIME.
YOU TOO, I UNDERSTAND.

GOT CAUGHT.
WHY'D IT HAPPEN?
MY TIME.
I FIND THAT HARD TO BELIEVE, WALTER. A MAN OF PREPAREDNESS AND RESOURCEFULNESS AS YOUR ARE.
COULD YOU SHED SOME LIGHT ON WHAT HAPPENED TO TAVON COAKLEY THE OTHER NIGHT?
HE FELL.
ACCORDING TO THIS REPORT, THAT WOULD MEAN HE FELL ON A PAIR OF TEETH, WHICH SOMEHOW PENETRATED HIS BRAIN THROUGH HIS ORBITAL CAVITIES.
TRAGIC.
HOW'S THAT DENTAL WORK THESE DAYS, WALTER?

OFFICERS, COULD YOU BOTH STEP OUTSIDE FOR A MOMENT?
YES SIR. KNOCK ON THE DOOR ONCE YOU'RE DONE.
SURE.
YOU'RE NOT MAKING THINGS EASY FOR ME, WALTER.
I'M TRYING TO HELP YOU, BUT YOU NEED TO HELP ME UNDERSTAND WHAT IT IS YOU WANT.
FUCK YOU.
I ALREADY KNOW WHO YOU ARE FROM YOUR FILE, WHAT I DON'T KNOW IS--
YOU KNOW SHIT.
YOU KNOW AS MUCH ABOUT ME AS I WANT YOU TO KNOW.
I ALREADY KNOW MORE ABOUT YOU IN TEN MINUTES THAN YOU KNOW ABOUT ME FROM THAT FILE... CAPTAIN.

IMPRESS ME.
YOUR ACCENT TELLS ME YOU'RE FROM THE MIDWEST - IOWA, ILLINOIS MAYBE.
THE PATHETIC INTERROGATION TECHNIQUES POINT TO SPECIAL OPS, THOUGH THE GREEN BERETS TEACH THE SAME KIND OF USELESS SHIT.
YOU ALSO HAVE A FAMILY. AND A CHILD... A GIRL, I'D SAY.
THAT'S ENOUGH. WE'RE HERE TO TALK ABOUT YOU.
FINE. WANT TO TALK ABOUT ME?
I HAD A LITTLE GIRL ONCE. HER NAME WAS SAMANTHA.
AND THESE PEOPLE YOU'RE STOPPING ME FROM KILLING AR THE ONES THAT TOOK HER FROM ME.
GOD'S PLAN GIVES ME THE STRENGTH AND VIRTUE TO PREVENT THESE SCUM-BAGS FROM BREATHING UP ALL THE OXYGEN MY DAUGHTER WON'T EVER GET TO.
YOU CAN SIT HERE AND JUDGE ME, CAPTAIN... BUT YOU AND I ARE THE SAME.
ONLY ONE BAD DAY SEPARATES YOU FROM BECOMING ME.
JUST ONE.
BAD.
DAY.
DO NOT LACK THE VIRTUE TO ACT, CAPTAIN.
IF YOU REALLY WANT TO KNOW WHO I AM...
...THEN DO THE LORD'S WORK. HELP ME DESTROY THEM.
BAMSUN
MASTER

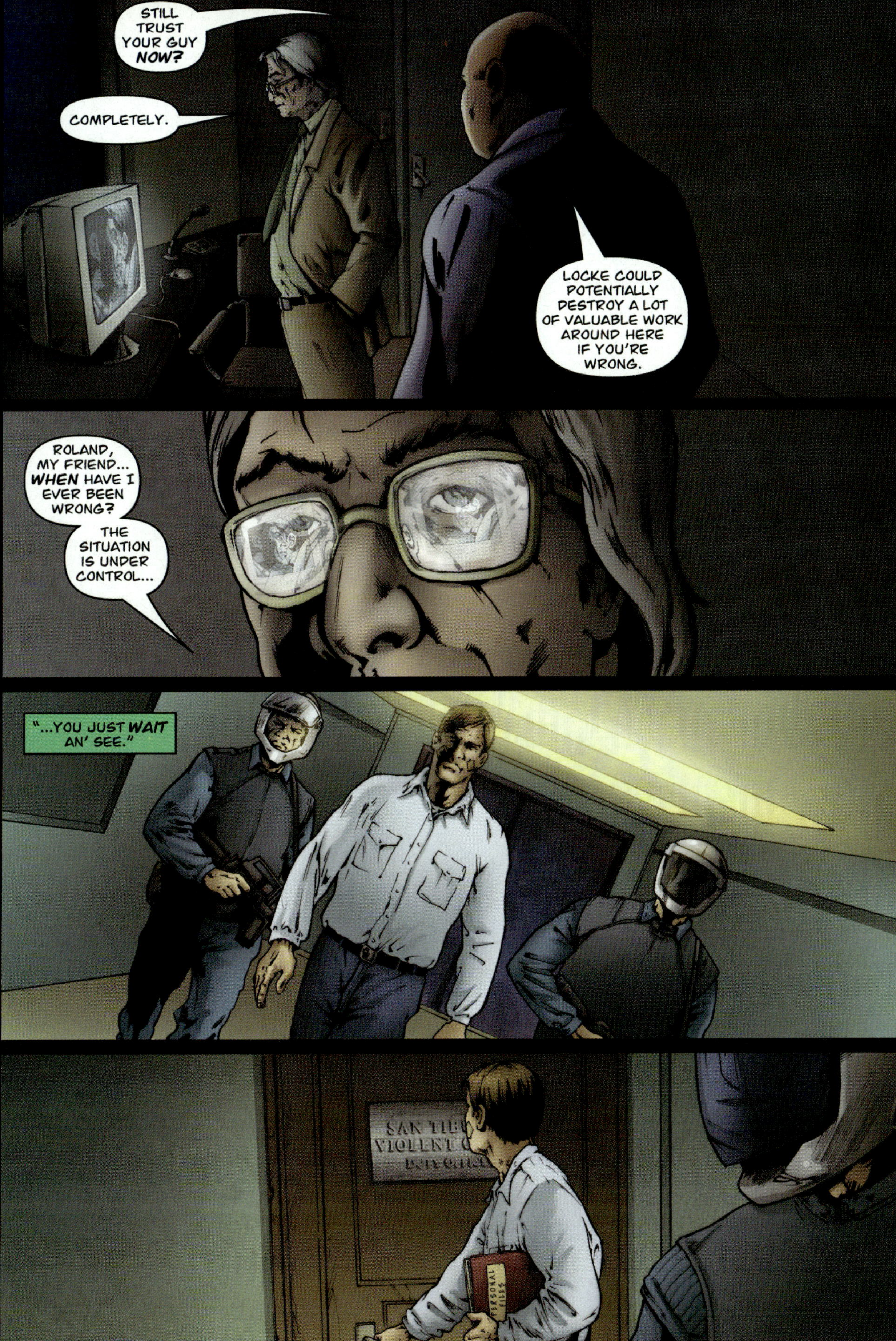
STILL TRUST YOUR GUY NOW?
COMPLETELY.
LOCKE COULD POTENTIALLY DESTROY A LOT OF VALUABLE WORK AROUND HERE IF YOU'RE WRONG.
ROLAND, MY FRIEND... WHEN HAVE I EVER BEEN WRONG?
THE SITUATION IS UNDER CONTROL...
"...YOU JUST WAIT AN' SEE."

LOCKE'S OFFER MAKES SENSE.
WHAT HE'S SUGGESTING WOULDN'T BE EASY. IT WOULD REQUIRE A LOT OF COMPLEX PLANNING AND PLANNED COINCIDENCE.
AND I'D BE A PARTY IN THE CONSPIRACY TO COMMIT MURDER.
BUT IF THE PEOPLE WE KILL REALLY AND TRULY DESERVED TO DIE... WHAT THEN?
ARE SOME OF THESE PEOPLE ONLY *ALIVE* BY VIRTUE OF THE FACT NO ONE HAS EFFICENTLY JUDGED THEM?
RIGHT OR WRONG... MY CHOICE IS MADE.
I'M IN.
AND NOW I HAVE TO SEE IT THROUGH.
FAITH BE UNTO THEE... CAPTAIN.

JASON! HOW WAS YOUR FIRST NIGHT IN THE TANK?
IT'S DEFINITELY GOING TO TAKE SOME GETTING USED TO, SIR.
ALL IN DUE TIME. JASON, THIS IS ASSISTANT WARDEN ROLAND PETTIBONE.
A PLEASURE, SIR.
YOU'LL EXCUSE ME IF I LEAVE YOU AND YOUR... PROTEGE HERE TO YOUR OWN DEVICES.
I'VE HEARD A LOT OF THINGS ABOUT YOU, MISTER BRODY.
SOME OF THEM ARE EVEN TRUE.
WELCOME ABOARD.

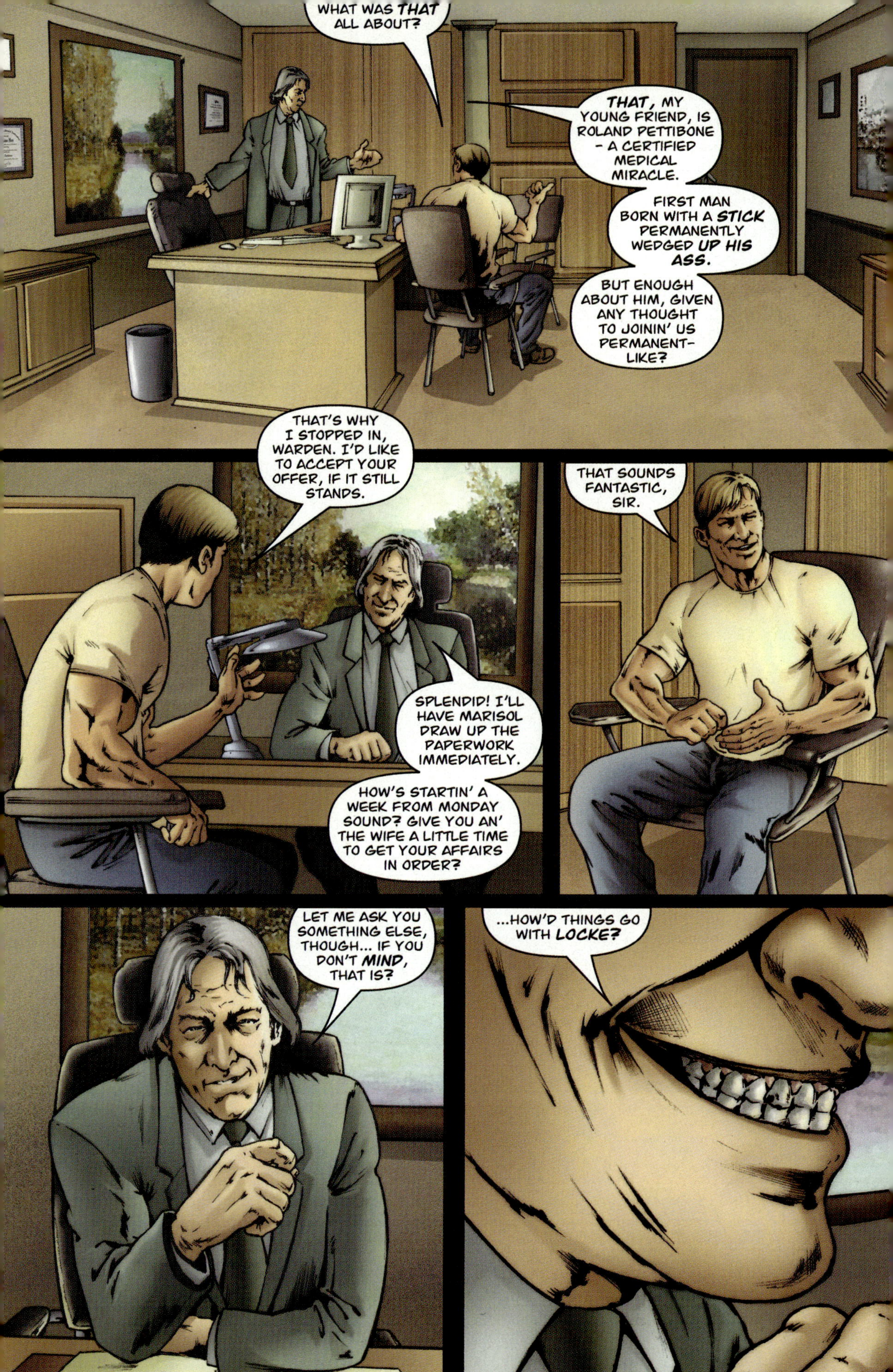
WHAT WAS THAT ALL ABOUT?
THAT, MY YOUNG FRIEND, IS ROLAND PETTIBONE - A CERTIFIED MEDICAL MIRACLE.
FIRST MAN BORN WITH A STICK PERMANENTLY WEDGED UP HIS ASS.
BUT ENOUGH ABOUT HIM, GIVEN ANY THOUGHT TO JOININ' US PERMANENT-LIKE?
THAT'S WHY I STOPPED IN, WARDEN. I'D LIKE TO ACCEPT YOUR OFFER, IF IT STILL STANDS.
SPLENDID! I'LL HAVE MARISOL DRAW UP THE PAPERWORK IMMEDIATELY.
HOW'S STARTIN' A WEEK FROM MONDAY SOUND? GIVE YOU AN' THE WIFE A LITTLE TIME TO GET YOUR AFFAIRS IN ORDER?
THAT SOUNDS FANTASTIC, SIR.
LET ME ASK YOU SOMETHING ELSE, THOUGH... IF YOU DON'T MIND, THAT IS?
...HOW'D THINGS GO WITH LOCKE?

MY ASSESSMENT OF LOCKE IS THAT HE'S COMPLETELY OUT OF TOUCH WITH ANY SEMBLANCE OF REALITY.
HIS SITUATION WILL NEED TO BE ADDRESSED IMMEDIATELY IF WE'RE GOING TO PREVENT FUTURE PROBLEMS.
...GO ON.
AND I TAKE IT YOU HAVE SOME SUGGESTIONS ON HOW TO... REMEDY THIS SITUATION?
WARDEN, IF I'M GOING TO BE TAKING OVER THE UNIT... I NEED TO KNOW I'LL HAVE FULL CONTROL TO ADDRESS ISSUES OF SAFETY IN MY WING.
Augusta
Hilton Head Island
Savannah
Atlantic Ocean
Freeport City
Green Turtle Cay
299 mi
LOCKE WANTS TO TAKE ON VIOLENT CRIMINALS.

"...I SAY WE GIVE HIM WHAT HE WANTS."
SHSSHSHHH
SHSSHH--
DON'T BE AFRAID, WALTER.
IT'S JUST THAT I'VE BEEN THINKING ABOUT WHAT YOU SAID. ABOUT THE TWO OF US BEING THE SAME...

THE TRUTH IS, LOCKE... WE'RE NOT THE SAME.
BECAUSE UNLIKE YOU, I HAVE THE STRENGTH OF WILL TO MAKE THE HARD CHOICES IN LIFE.
ONLY GOD CAN JUDGE ME
THE CAPACITY TO CUT OFF A FINGER... TO SAVE THE HAND.
THE VIRTUE, I THINK YOU SAID.
AND THAT'S SOMETHING A PIECE OF SHIT LIKE YOU WILL NEVER UNDERSTAND.

SIR, WE HAVE A SITUATION.
DOES IT INVOLVE PEOPLE BARGING INTO YOUR OFFICE WITHOUT KNOCKING?
BECAUSE IT'S AN EPIDEMIC AROUND HERE.
VIOLENT CRIME
SHOWER FACILITY.
MOVE OUT OF THE WAY!
...MULTIPLE FRACTURES AND INTERNAL HEMORRHAGING, I NEED 10-CC'S OF MORPHINE IN HERE STAT, AND A MEDICAL TEAM READY FOR IMMEDIATE SURGERY ON A COLLAPSED LUNG...
MOVE IT FOLKS! HE DOESN'T HAVE MUCH TIME!
PAYBACK WAS A BITCH
OHH, JASON...
...YOU AND ME'S GONNA GET ALONG JUST FINE. BOY. JUST FINE INDEED...
"All virtue is summed up in dealing justly"
-Aristotle, 384-322

CHAPTER 3

CORRECTIVE
MEASURES

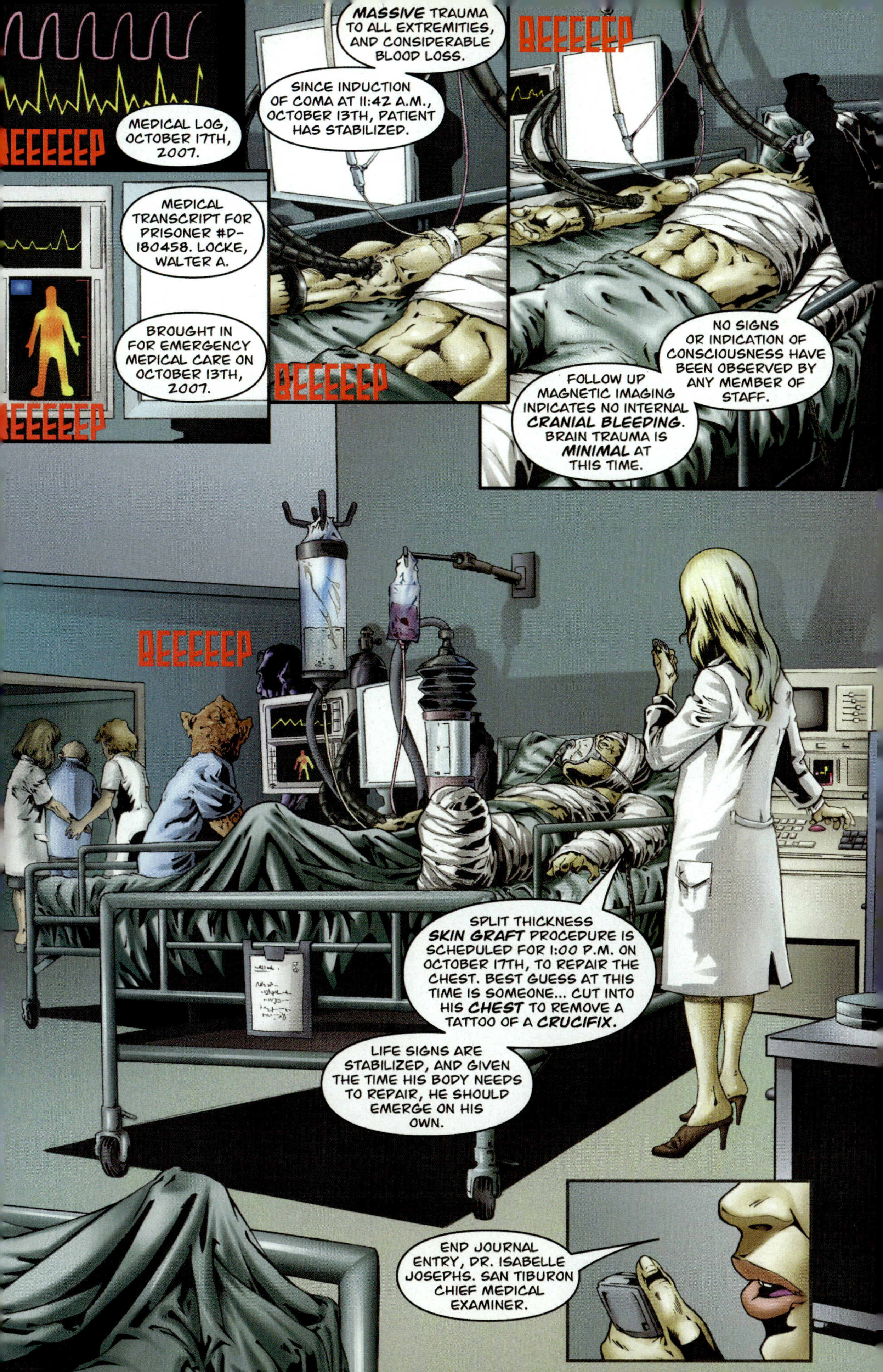

MEDICAL LOG, OCTOBER 17TH, 2007.
MEDICAL TRANSCRIPT FOR PRISONER #D-180458. LOCKE, WALTER A.
BROUGHT IN FOR EMERGENCY MEDICAL CARE ON OCTOBER 13TH, 2007.
MASSIVE TRAUMA TO ALL EXTREMITIES, AND CONSIDERABLE BLOOD LOSS.
SINCE INDUCTION OF COMA AT 11:42 A.M., OCTOBER 13TH, PATIENT HAS STABILIZED.
BEEEEEP
BEEEEEP
NO SIGNS OR INDICATION OF CONSCIOUSNESS HAVE BEEN OBSERVED BY ANY MEMBER OF STAFF.
FOLLOW UP MAGNETIC IMAGING INDICATES NO INTERNAL CRANIAL BLEEDING. BRAIN TRAUMA IS MINIMAL AT THIS TIME.
BEEEEEP
SPLIT THICKNESS SKIN GRAFT PROCEDURE IS SCHEDULED FOR 1:00 P.M. ON OCTOBER 17TH, TO REPAIR THE CHEST. BEST GUESS AT THIS TIME IS SOMEONE... CUT INTO HIS CHEST TO REMOVE A TATTOO OF A CRUCIFIX.
LIFE SIGNS ARE STABILIZED, AND GIVEN THE TIME HIS BODY NEEDS TO REPAIR, HE SHOULD EMERGE ON HIS OWN.
END JOURNAL ENTRY, DR. ISABELLE JOSEPHS. SAN TIBURON CHIEF MEDICAL EXAMINER.

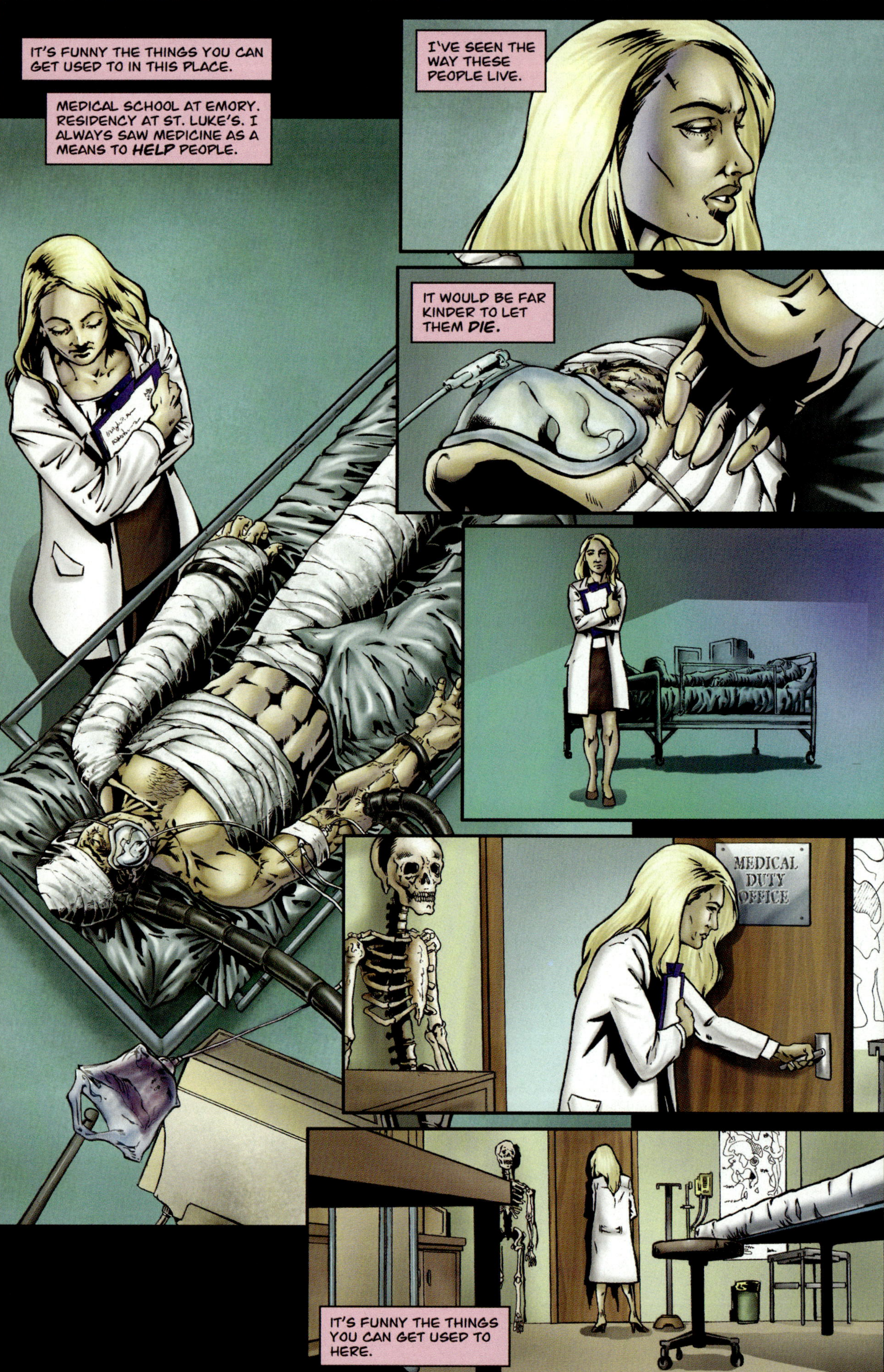
IT'S FUNNY THE THINGS YOU CAN GET USED TO IN THIS PLACE.
MEDICAL SCHOOL AT EMORY. RESIDENCY AT ST. LUKE'S. I ALWAYS SAW MEDICINE AS A MEANS TO HELP PEOPLE.
I'VE SEEN THE WAY THESE PEOPLE LIVE.
IT WOULD BE FAR KINDER TO LET THEM DIE.
MEDICAL DUTY OFFICE
IT'S FUNNY THE THINGS YOU CAN GET USED TO HERE.

AND NOT FUNNY AT ALL THE THINGS YOU CAN'T.
BUT THAT'S THE PRICE YOU PAY FOR TAKING THE OATH.
POWERLESS
STORY * PENCILS * COLORS * LETTERS
Grant Chastain * Fran Moyano * Jay Moyano * Mike Storniolo

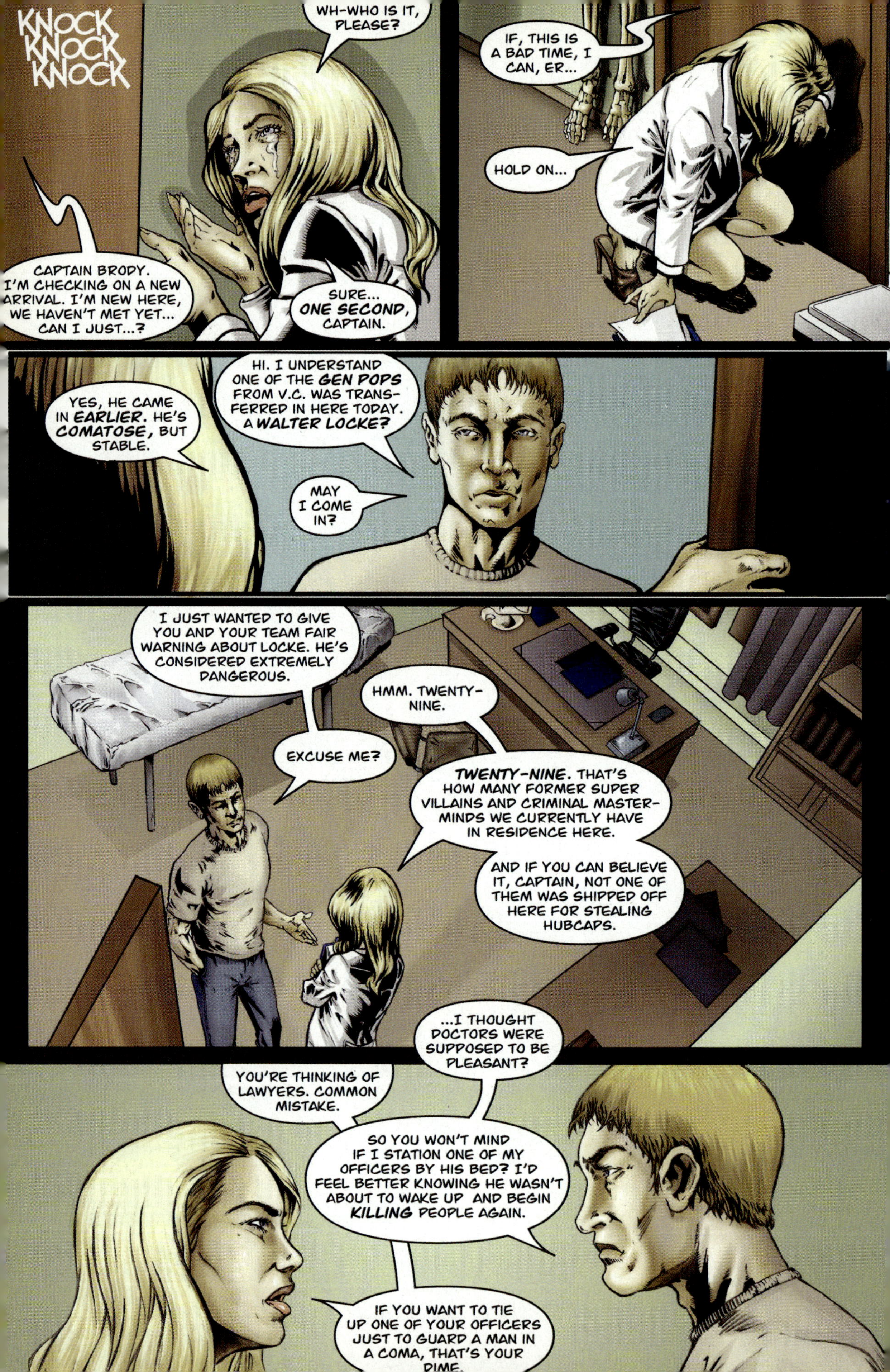
KNOCK KNOCK KNOCK
WH-WHO IS IT, PLEASE?
CAPTAIN BRODY. I'M CHECKING ON A NEW ARRIVAL. I'M NEW HERE, WE HAVEN'T MET YET... CAN I JUST...?
SURE... ONE SECOND, CAPTAIN.
IF, THIS IS A BAD TIME, I CAN, ER...
HOLD ON...
HI. I UNDERSTAND ONE OF THE GEN POPS FROM V.C. WAS TRANSFERRED IN HERE TODAY. A WALTER LOCKE?
YES, HE CAME IN EARLIER. HE'S COMATOSE, BUT STABLE.
MAY I COME IN?
I JUST WANTED TO GIVE YOU AND YOUR TEAM FAIR WARNING ABOUT LOCKE. HE'S CONSIDERED EXTREMELY DANGEROUS.
HMM. TWENTY-NINE.
EXCUSE ME?
TWENTY-NINE. THAT'S HOW MANY FORMER SUPER VILLAINS AND CRIMINAL MASTERMINDS WE CURRENTLY HAVE IN RESIDENCE HERE.
AND IF YOU CAN BELIEVE IT, CAPTAIN, NOT ONE OF THEM WAS SHIPPED OFF HERE FOR STEALING HUBCAPS.
...I THOUGHT DOCTORS WERE SUPPOSED TO BE PLEASANT?
YOU'RE THINKING OF LAWYERS. COMMON MISTAKE.
SO YOU WON'T MIND IF I STATION ONE OF MY OFFICERS BY HIS BED? I'D FEEL BETTER KNOWING HE WASN'T ABOUT TO WAKE UP AND BEGIN KILLING PEOPLE AGAIN.
IF YOU WANT TO TIE UP ONE OF YOUR OFFICERS JUST TO GUARD A MAN IN A COMA, THAT'S YOUR DIME.

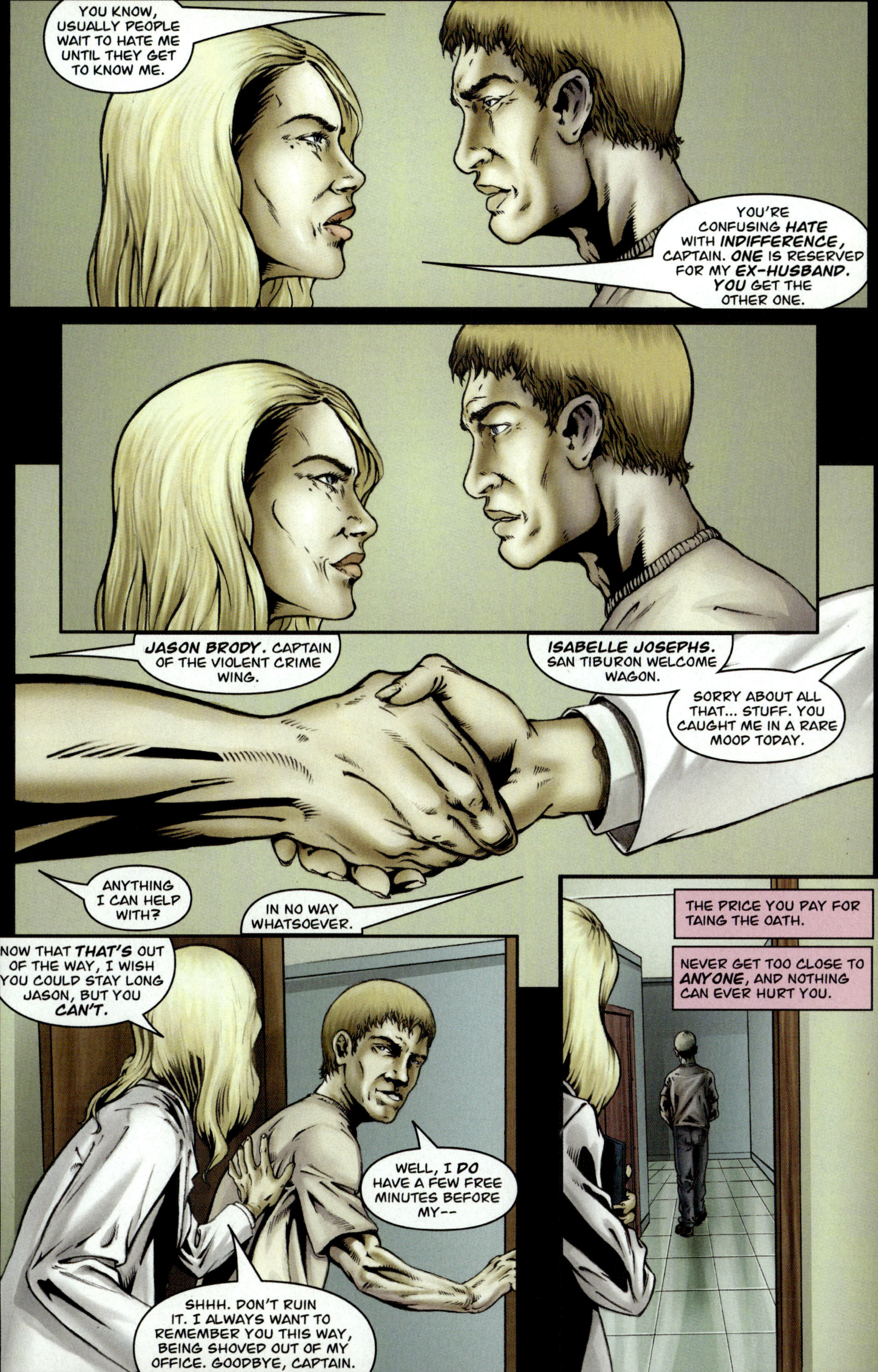

YOU KNOW, USUALLY PEOPLE WAIT TO HATE ME UNTIL THEY GET TO KNOW ME.
YOU'RE CONFUSING **HATE** WITH **INDIFFERENCE**, CAPTAIN. **ONE** IS RESERVED FOR MY **EX-HUSBAND. YOU** GET THE OTHER ONE.
JASON BRODY. CAPTAIN OF THE VIOLENT CRIME WING.
ISABELLE JOSEPHS. SAN TIBURON WELCOME WAGON.
SORRY ABOUT ALL THAT... STUFF. YOU CAUGHT ME IN A RARE MOOD TODAY.
ANYTHING I CAN HELP WITH?
IN NO WAY WHATSOEVER.
NOW THAT **THAT'S** OUT OF THE WAY, I WISH YOU COULD STAY LONG JASON, BUT YOU **CAN'T.**
WELL, I **DO** HAVE A FEW FREE MINUTES BEFORE MY--
SHHH. DON'T RUIN IT. I ALWAYS WANT TO REMEMBER YOU THIS WAY, BEING SHOVED OUT OF MY OFFICE. GOODBYE, CAPTAIN.
THE PRICE YOU PAY FOR TAING THE OATH.
NEVER GET TOO CLOSE TO **ANYONE**, AND NOTHING CAN EVER HURT YOU.

DEVLIN GIVES ME THE NEXT THREE DAYS OFF TO TAKE CARE OF PERSONAL AFFAIRS. FIND A HOUSE, SEE ABOUT DAY CARE, FORWARD THE MAIL.
I SHOULD BE WORRIED. THOSE THINGS TAKE TIME AND CAREFUL PLANNING. MUCH LONGER THAN A WEEK.
BUT I CAN'T EVEN THINK THAT FAR AHEAD.
ALL I WANT AND NEED RIGHT NOW IS AN HOUR AWAY, WAITING FOR ME AT THE DOCKS.
EVERYTHING I'LL EVER WANT AND NEED.
AND JUST LIKE THAT, THE MILES DISSOLVE. THE HOURS PASS. THE AIR GETS THIN.

AND EVERYTHING ELSE JUST FALLS AWAY.
WELCOME DADY
DA DA!
YOU MISSED US.
GUILTY AS CHARGED.
YOU ARE SO WHIPPED.
HEY, WHAT CAN I SAY? AROUND YOU...

"...I GUESS I'M JUST POWERLESS."
MISTER CARMICHAEL, PLEASE FACE THE CAMERA, AND HOLD UP THE SIGN BOARD.
#C-217493
I-IS THERE SOMEONE HERE I CAN SPEAK WITH? THERE'S... THERE'S BEEN A BIT OF A --
POOMF
I DON'T WANT TO- ER, IS THERE A SUPERVISOR OF SOME--
TURN TO YOUR RIGHT.
CLIK-WRRRRR
SEE, I'M NOT REALLY- I DON'T NEED THIS NECKLACE ON, I DON'T HAVE ANY--
TURN TO YOUR RIGHT, SIR.
ARE WE CLEAR?
ALL RIGHT! OK, JUST DON'T- SHOOT ME, JESUS. THERE'S BEEN A BIG MISTAKE.
HOLD FOR THE PICTURE.
ARE ANY OF YOU LISTENING TO ME? PLEASE, I SAID I DON'T HAVE--
POOMF
CLIK-WRRRRR
"SO, YOU SEE, SIR, I'M NOT REALLY SUPPOSED TO BE HERE AT ALL. BIG MISUNDERSTANDING, I'M AFRAID."
#C-217493

clayton. Carmichael
LARCEN
clayton. Carmichael
LARCEN. nº #C-217493
#C-217493
He was sentenced to 15 years at
Tiburon for:
Grand Larceny, Conspiracy, Extortion,
Racketeering, and Attempted Murder.
SIGH
MISTAH CARMICHAEL, PERHAPS YOU CAN...ENLIGHTEN ME AS TO THE REASON I'M SEEING YOU TODAY?
YOU DO REALIZE, I DON'T MAKE THE RULES ABOUT WHERE YOU GET SENT.
I UNDERSTAND THAT, SIR. IT'S JUST... WELL, I SIMPLY CAN'T STAY HERE. THIS FACILITY, THIS NECKLACE, THEY'RE-- WELL, THEY'RE NOT FOR ME.
OH, REALLY NOW.
WELL, THIS FACILITY IS FOR SUPERPOWERED CRIMINALS. NOW, I MIGHT HAVE BEEN A CRIMINAL, THAT MUCH I'LL ADMIT- BUT I DON'T ACTUALLY POSSESS INNATE POWERS.
MY SKILLS, IF YOU WILL, WERE THE PRODUCT OF A SUB-ETHER CLOAKING AND SOUND DAMPENING BELTED DEVICE THAT I NO LONGER HAVE IN MY POSSESSION.
PUTTING ME IN HERE WOULD CONSTITUTE A VIOLATION OF MY HUMAN RIGHTS. SO, WELL, TO MAKE A LONG STORY SHORT, I'D APPRECIATE IF WE COULD MOVE FOR AN IMMEDIATE TRANSFER?
UHM, OK?

=SIGH=
THREE THINGS, MISTAH CARMICHAEL...
NUMBAH ONE, FUNNY STORIES BEGIN WITH "THERE ONCE WAS A MAN FROM" OR "WHAT DO YOU GET WHEN YOU CROSS A". ANYTHING ELSE IS A BORING WASTE OF MY FUCKING TIME!
NUMBAH TWO, DON'T YOU EVER CALL ME SIR. YOU IGNORANT, SHIT-EATING LITTLE COCKSUCKER. YOU ARE A SCUM-BAG AND HAVEN'T YET EARNED THE RIGHT TO REFER TO ME IN A FAMILIAR WAY.
IF I EVER DESIGN TO ENGAGE YOU IN COVERSATION AGAIN, I WILL BE REFERED TO AS "WARDEN", "WARDEN DEVLIN" OR THE MUCH PREFERRED "GOD". ANY OTHER ABUSE OF MY NAME WILL RESULT IN THESE GENTLEMEN INTRODUCING YOU TO THE JOYS OF THE BRAINJOLT FEATURE OF YOUR FUCKIN' DOG COLLAR.
ANY QUESTIONS FROM THE FUCKIN' PEANUT GALLERY ON NUMBERS ONE OR TWO?!?
N-NO, WARDEN.
WARDEN WHAT?
WARDEN. WARDEN GOD. GOD WARDEN.

I LIKE THAT! WARDEN GOD. NUMBAH THREE, OTHERWISE KNOWN AS THE LAST PIECE OF WISDOM I'LL BE SHARING WITH YOU.
DON'T YOU EVER QUESTION ME.
I'VE READ YOUR FILE. YOU AIN'T GOT ONE PERSON **ALIVE** GIVES A **FUCK** WHAT HAPPENS TO YOU. SO DON'T BE THINKIN' YOU'RE GOING TO CALL DOWN THE WRATH OF ACLU OR THE GOV'MENT.
CAUSE I CAN PROMISE YOU, YOU'LL BE DEAD AN' GONE BY THE TIME THEY EVEN THINK TO WONDER WHAT HAPPENED TO YOUR NARROW ASS.
NO QUESTIONS? GOOD. GENTLEMEN, TAKE MISTAH CARMICHAEL HERE TO HIS NEW LUXURY SUITE. HELP HIM GET ACCLIMATED.
BUT, ***I DON'T HAVE ANY POWERS!*** I'M NOT- HOW CAN- HOW AM I SUPPOSED-
SAME WAY EVERY-ONE ELSE DOES. KICK SOMEBODY'S ASS, JOIN THE ARYAN BROTHERHOOD, OR SUCK A DICK. ONE WAY OR ANOTHER, YOU'LL ADJUST.
LOOK ON THE BRIGHT SIDE, MISTAH CARMICHAEL, ONLY FOURTEEN YEARS AND 364 MORE DAYS, AND YOU'LL BE ELIGIBLE FOR PAROLE!
I'LL CHECK IN WITH HIM LATER.
YOU'RE LOVING THIS, AREN'T YOU?
HAVE A PLEASANT MORNING, ***WARDEN GOD.***
HEH
BALD DICK-HEAD.

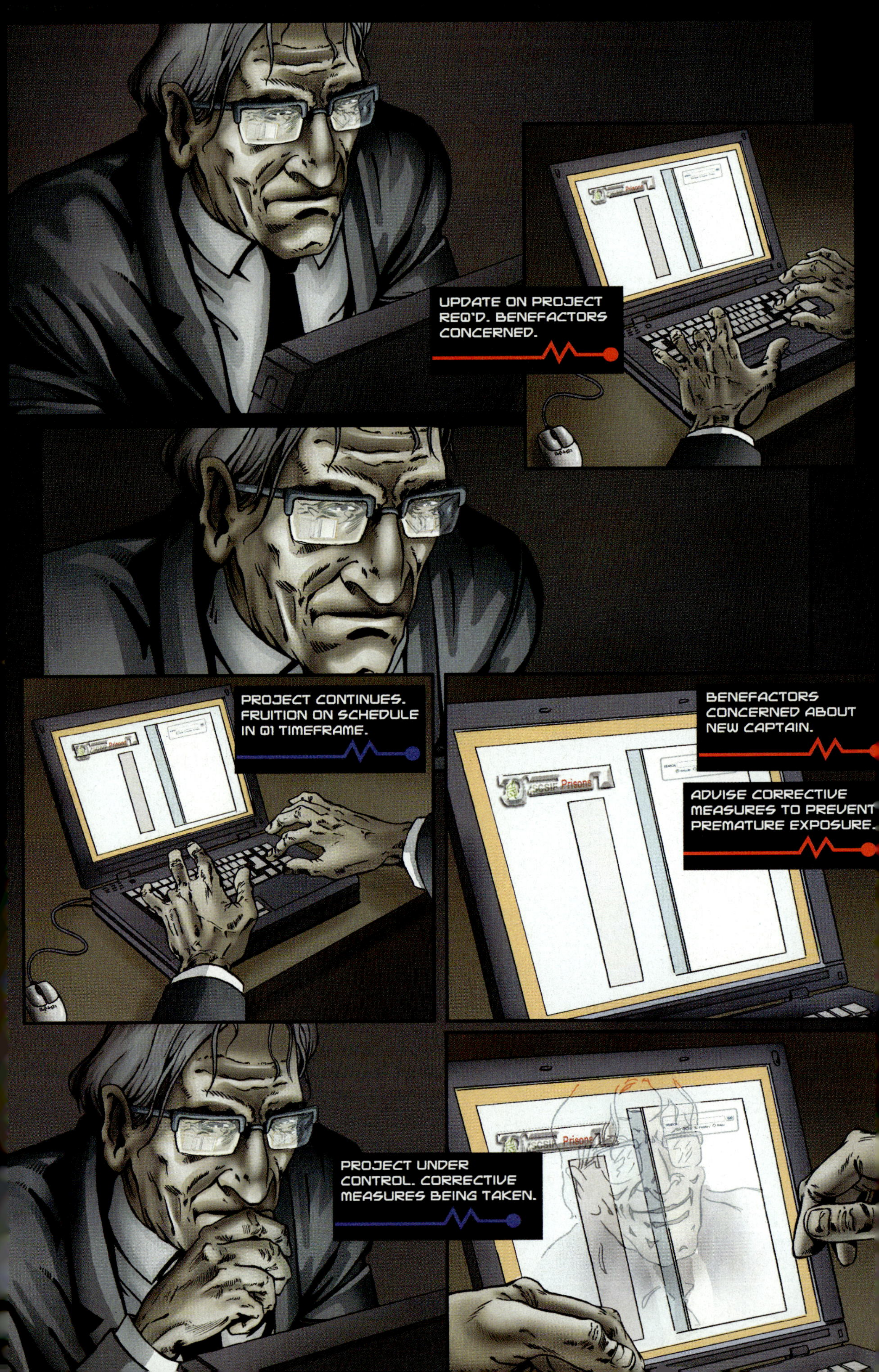
UPDATE ON PROJECT
REQ'D. BENEFACTORS
CONCERNED.
PROJECT CONTINUES.
FRUITION ON SCHEDULE
IN Q1 TIMEFRAME.
BENEFACTORS
CONCERNED ABOUT
NEW CAPTAIN.
ADVISE CORRECTIVE
MEASURES TO PREVENT
PREMATURE EXPOSURE.
PROJECT UNDER
CONTROL. CORRECTIVE
MEASURES BEING TAKEN.

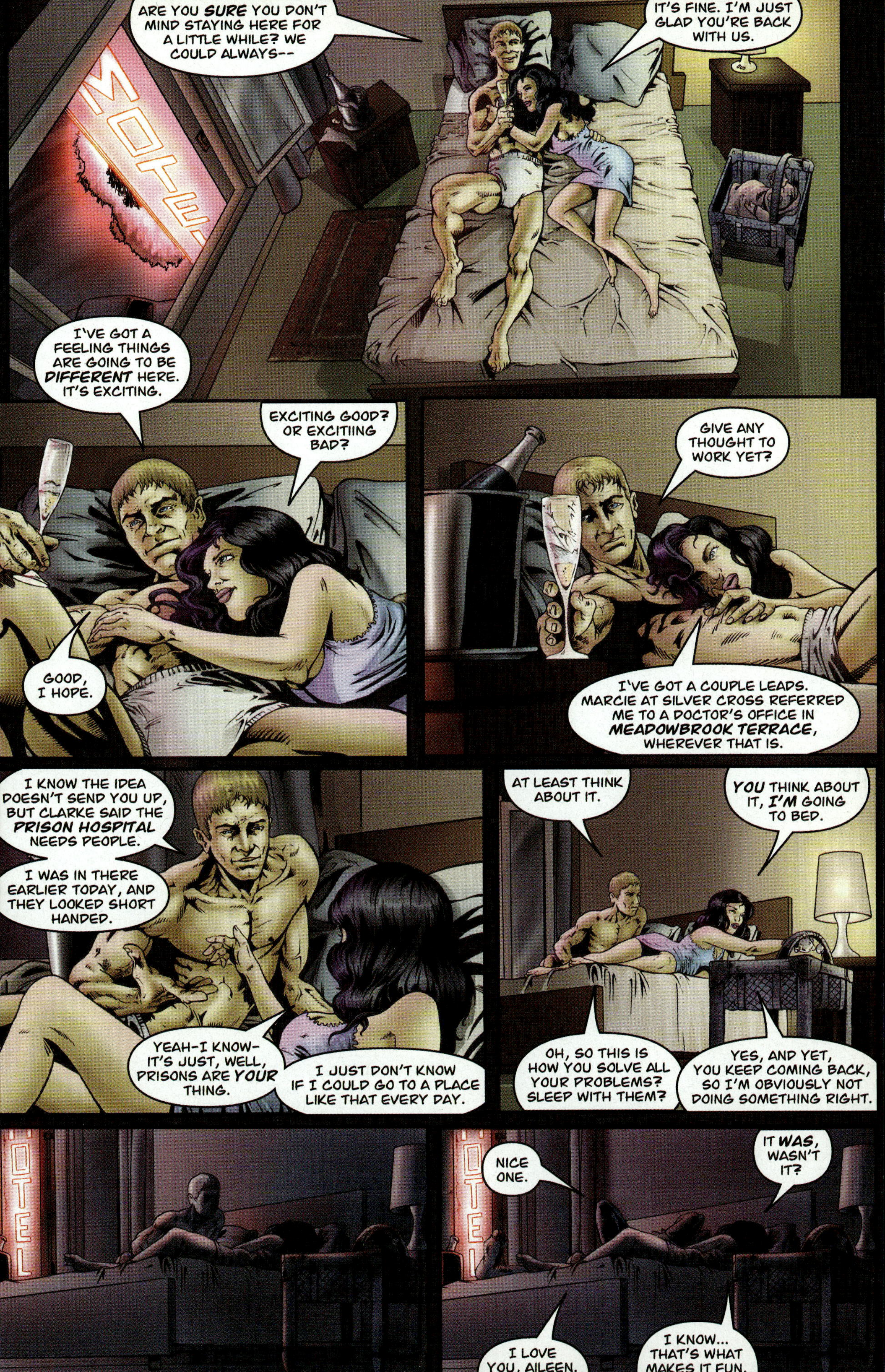
ARE YOU **SURE** YOU DON'T MIND STAYING HERE FOR A LITTLE WHILE? WE COULD ALWAYS--
IT'S FINE. I'M JUST GLAD YOU'RE BACK WITH US.
MOTEL
I'VE GOT A FEELING THINGS ARE GOING TO BE **DIFFERENT** HERE. IT'S EXCITING.
EXCITING GOOD? OR EXCITIING BAD?
GOOD, I HOPE.
GIVE ANY THOUGHT TO WORK YET?
I'VE GOT A COUPLE LEADS. MARCIE AT SILVER CROSS REFERRED ME TO A DOCTOR'S OFFICE IN **MEADOWBROOK TERRACE,** WHEREVER THAT IS.
I KNOW THE IDEA DOESN'T SEND YOU UP, BUT CLARKE SAID THE **PRISON HOSPITAL** NEEDS PEOPLE.
I WAS IN THERE EARLIER TODAY, AND THEY LOOKED SHORT HANDED.
YEAH-I KNOW- IT'S JUST, WELL, PRISONS ARE **YOUR** THING.
I JUST DON'T KNOW IF I COULD GO TO A PLACE LIKE THAT EVERY DAY.
AT LEAST THINK ABOUT IT.
YOU THINK ABOUT IT, **I'M** GOING TO BED.
OH, SO THIS IS HOW YOU SOLVE ALL YOUR PROBLEMS? SLEEP WITH THEM?
YES, AND YET, YOU KEEP COMING BACK, SO I'M OBVIOUSLY NOT DOING SOMETHING RIGHT.
NICE ONE.
IT **WAS,** WASN'T IT?
I LOVE YOU, AILEEN.
I KNOW... THAT'S WHAT MAKES IT FUN.

FISH!
FISH!
FISH!
DO THEY
SAYING
HAT?
ISH!
FISH!
FISH!
FISH!
KEEP TO THE RIGHT, SIR.
FISH!
FISH!
FISH!
FISH!
FISH!
SERIOUSLY, Y'KNOW? WHAT'S WITH THE FISH? IS THAT A DINNER THING?
FISH!
ISH!
WHY WON'T YOU ANSWER ME?
FIS
PRISON REGULATIONS FORBID FRATERNIZATION WITH CSB'S.
FISH!
FISH!
FISH!
FISH!
FISH!
FISH!
CBS'S?
FISH!
FISH!
FISH!
CONTROL- POD DOOR RELEASE FOR UNIT ASSIGNED TO CHARLIE-TWO-ONE-SEVEN-FOUR-NINER-THREE.
FISH!
FISH!
FISH!
FISH!
FISH!
FISH!
COPY THAT, CONTROL.
WHOA!
FISH!
FISH!
FISH!
FISH!
FISH!
FISH!
FISH!
FISH!
I'M INNOCENT
WHA-HEY!
FISH!
C.S.B...
CONVICTED SHIT-BAG, IN OTHER WORDS... YOU!
ZERO SIX-THIRTY WAKEUP. PLEASANT DREAMS.
FISH!
FISH!
FISH!

WHY... WHY DO THEY-
FISH!
FISH!
FISH!
THIS GUPPY IS MINE, BOYS. I JUST LOVE SOME FINE WHITE MEAT.
FISH!
FISH!
FISH!
FISH!
FISH!
FISH!
FISH!
FISH!
FISH!
ONTROL, LIGHTS OUT N SECTOR V.C., GEN POP WING. ON YOUR MARK.
LIGHTS OUT, LADIES! SHUT THE FUCK UP!!
CARMICHAEL, YOU LUCKY ESE. CLEAVON THERE, WE CALL 'IM THE FUCKIN' MILK MAN. 'CUZ HE COMES IN LITTLE WHITE CANS!
HA! HA! HA! HA! HA!
PLEASANT DREAMS, SWEETIE!

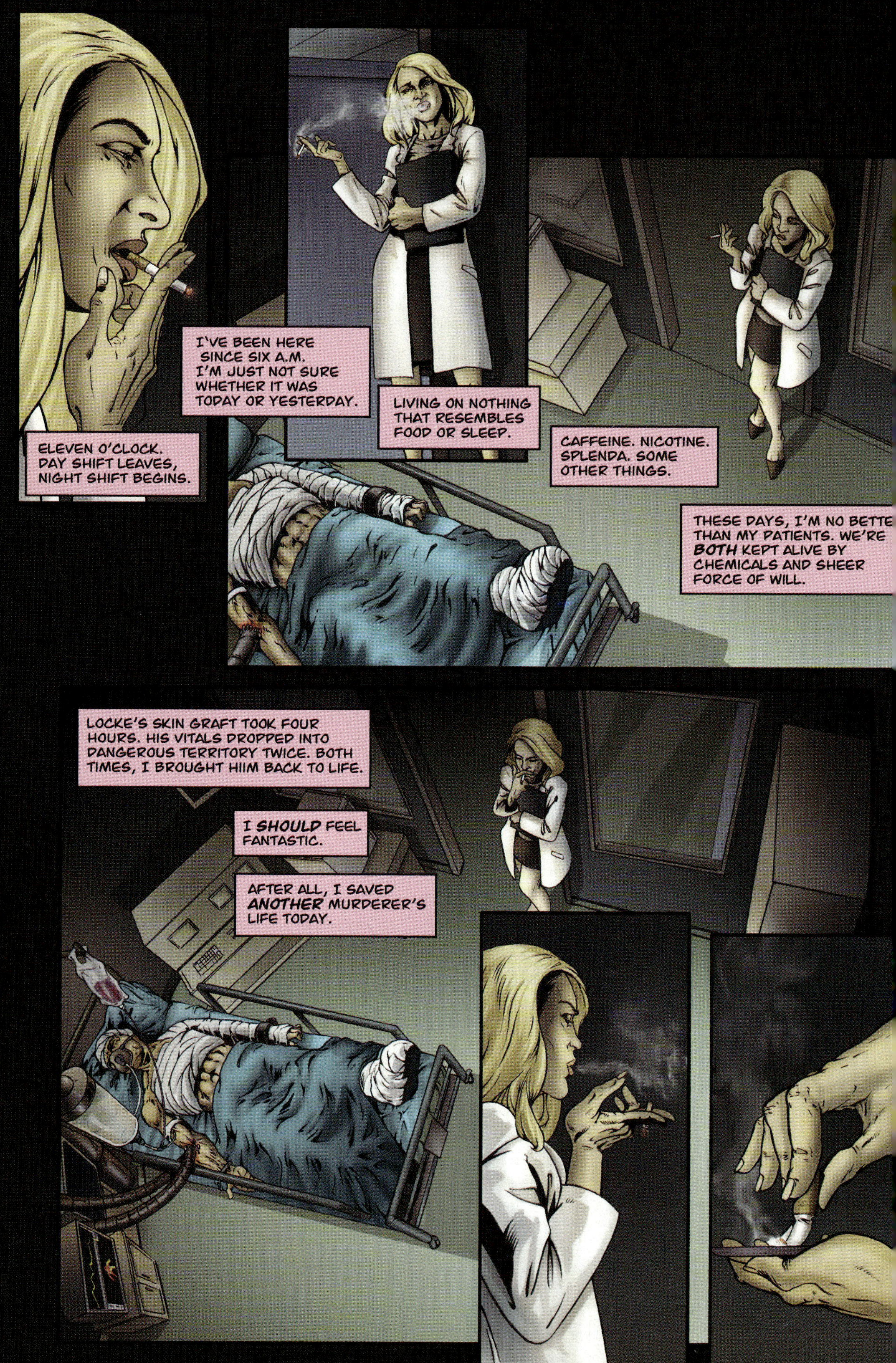

I'VE BEEN HERE SINCE SIX A.M. I'M JUST NOT SURE WHETHER IT WAS TODAY OR YESTERDAY.
ELEVEN O'CLOCK. DAY SHIFT LEAVES, NIGHT SHIFT BEGINS.
LIVING ON NOTHING THAT RESEMBLES FOOD OR SLEEP.
CAFFEINE. NICOTINE. SPLENDA. SOME OTHER THINGS.
THESE DAYS, I'M NO BETTE THAN MY PATIENTS. WE'RE **BOTH** KEPT ALIVE BY CHEMICALS AND SHEER FORCE OF WILL.
LOCKE'S SKIN GRAFT TOOK FOUR HOURS. HIS VITALS DROPPED INTO DANGEROUS TERRITORY TWICE. BOTH TIMES, I BROUGHT HIIM BACK TO LIFE.
I **SHOULD** FEEL FANTASTIC.
AFTER ALL, I SAVED **ANOTHER** MURDERER'S LIFE TODAY.

BZZZZZZZTTT
-CALL CODE BLUE, HE'S NOT CRASHING YET, BUT I WANT TO BE READY JUST IN CASE. JOHN, GET HIM PREPPED FOR THE O.R.
SIT REP?
NOTHING I CAN'T HANDLE, CHIEF.
TAKE HIM TO OPERATING ROOM 2, I CAN...
JOHN, WHEEL HIM DOWN, I'LL BE THERE SHORTLY.
DOCTOR, YOU'VE BEEN HERE SINCE SIX THIS MORNING, I'M THE SURGEON ON DUTY FOR THIS SHIFT, I'VE GOT THIS.
WE DON'T HAVE TIME FOR THIS, ANGIE, WE NEED--
WE'LL TALK ABOUT THIS LATER.
NO. WE DON'T HAVE TIME FOR THIS. I'M THE S.O.D. FOR THIS SHIFT, STOP FIGHTING ME, AND GET SOME REST. IF YOU THINK YOU CAN'T DO THAT, THEN OBSERVE.

ALL THE UNSPEAKABLE THINGS I'VE DONE...
MAYBE LOCKE WAS RIGHT ABOUT ME AFTER ALL.
MOTEL
MAYBE ALL IT TAKES FOR ANYBODY IS JUST ONE BAD DAY.

PARKING
MOTEL
"The exercise of power is determined by thousands of interactions..."

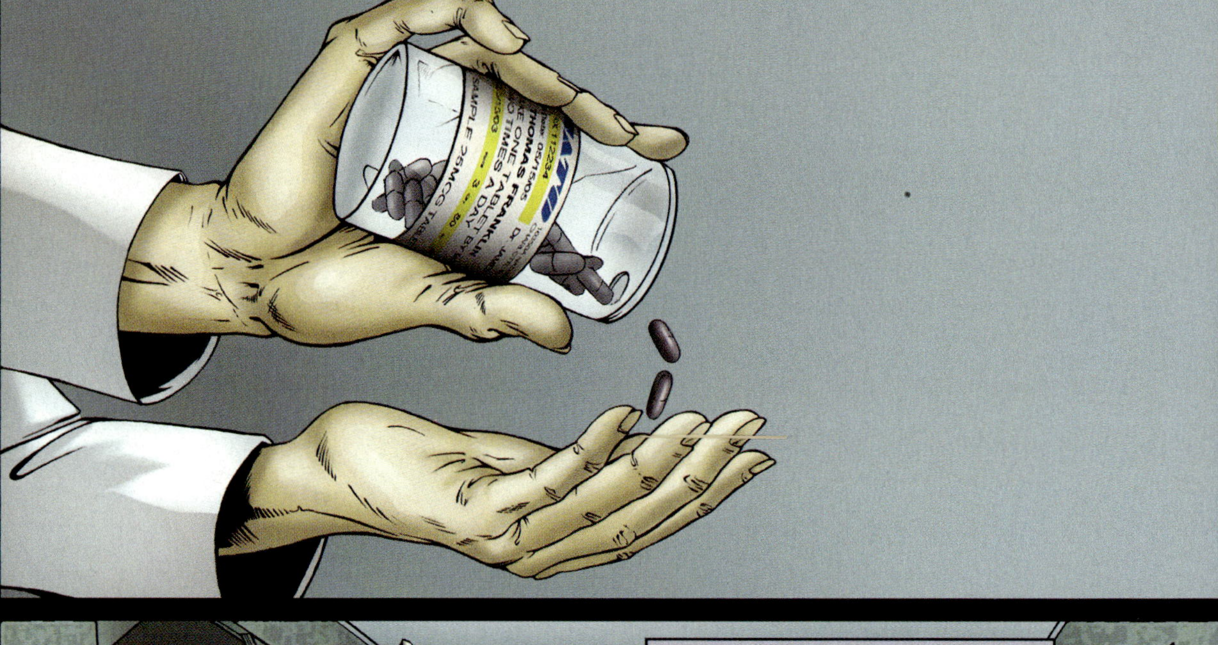

"...between the world of the POWERFUL, and the world of the POWERLESS..."

"...all the MORE so, because these worlds are never divided by a sharp line..."

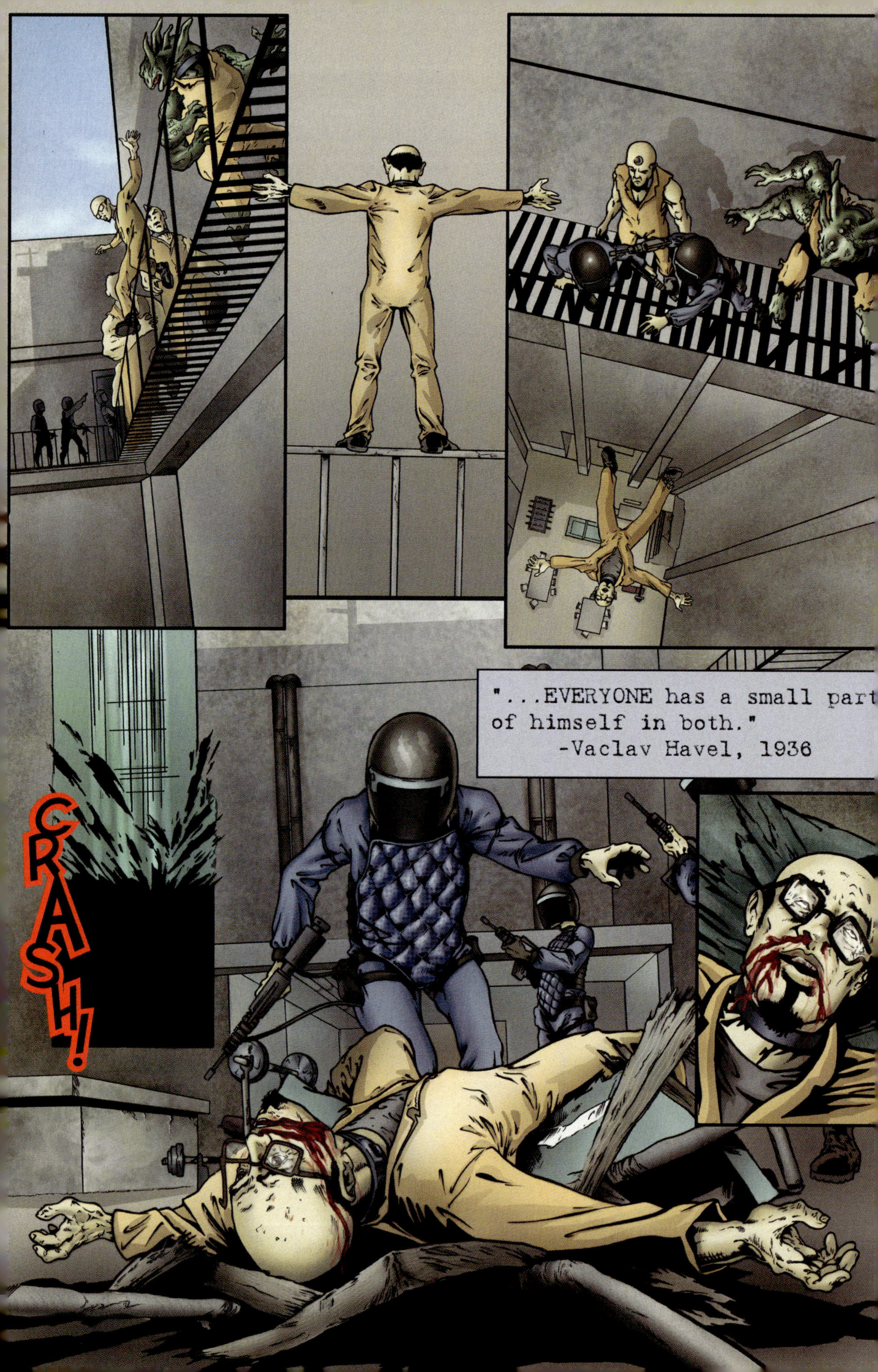
"...EVERYONE has a small part
of himself in both."
-Vaclav Havel, 1936
CRASH!

CHAPTER 4

CORRECTIVE MEASURES

MUNICIPAL BANK ROBBED BY "THE CONDUCTOR"!
2 DEAD, 5 INJURED.
OCTOBER 21, 1971
PHOTOGRAPHS AND MEMORIES ARE ALL THAT REMAINS OF MY YOUTH.

I HARDLY KNOW THAT KID IN THE PICTURE ANYMORE.
JUST SOME DUMB LITTLE ANIMAL WITH A MILLION DOLLAR'S WORTH OF POWER, WITH A BRAIN BOUGHT FOR LESS THAN A DIME.
EIGHT FEET TALL, AND BULLETPROOF.

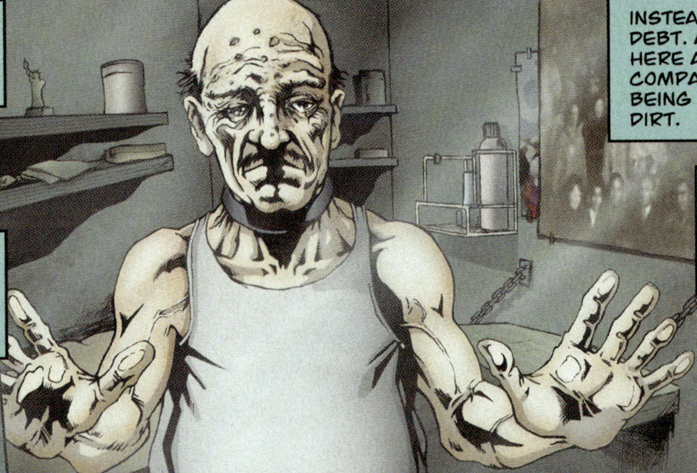
LOOKING BACK, I CAN'T SAY I'M SORRY FOR MUCH. STUPID KIDS DO STUPID THINGS.
THAT'S NO HEADLINE.
I COULDA ENDED UP LIKE THE CRETIN OR JOHNNY TWICE; DEAD AND FORGOTTEN IN A PINE BOX.
A NICE STONE MARKER NOBODY'S EVER GONNA READ.
INSTEAD, I PAID MY DEBT. AND STUCK IN HERE AIN'T SO BAD IN COMPARISON TO BEING STUCK THE DIRT.
THREE SQUARE MEALS. CABLE TV. THE ODD CARD GAME WITH DIAMOND JIM AND HIS CRONIES.

THE NAME'S GORDON TWEEDY. A LIFETIME AGO, I PUT ON A FRUITY LITTLE SUPER SUIT AND CALLED MYSELF "THE CONDUCTOR".
I'VE BEEN AT SAN TIBURON SINCE JANUARY, 1980. GOING ON TWENTY-EIGHT YEARS NOW.
AND TODAY... I'M UP FOR PAROLE.

JUMP!
JUMP!
JUMP!
JUMP!
MARY MOTHER OF GOD...
SINGLE-FILE TO THE MESS HALL, LADIES!
FIRST ONE 'A YOU WITH A WISE IDEA GETS A BRAIN JOLT AN' A BULLET!
NOT EVERYONE GETS A SECOND CHANCE.
AND NOT EVERYONE KNOWS WHAT TO DO WHEN THEY GET ONE.

I'VE LEARNED A LOT IN THIS PLACE.
FIRST OF ALL, LET ME TELL YOU ABOUT HOPE.
FUCK WHAT THAT SHINE MORGAN WHATSHISNAME SAID ABOUT HOPE IN THAT ONE MOVIE. YOU CAN'T SURVIVE IN A PLACE LIKE THIS WITHOUT IT.
LAST TWO WEEKS, THERE'S BEEN A MURDER, A SUICIDE, AND A PRETTY NOTORIOUS CASE OF VIGILANTE SHOWER JUSTICE.
PLUS, THE CAFETERIA JUST STARTED SERVING THESE SHITTY NEW BREAKFAST BARS.
EAT ONE 'A THEM SOMETIME- YOU'LL REALLY KNOW WHAT HOPE IS.
REFORMED
STORY * PENCILS * COLORS * LETTERS
Grant Chastain * Fran Moyano * Jay Moyano * Mike Storniolo

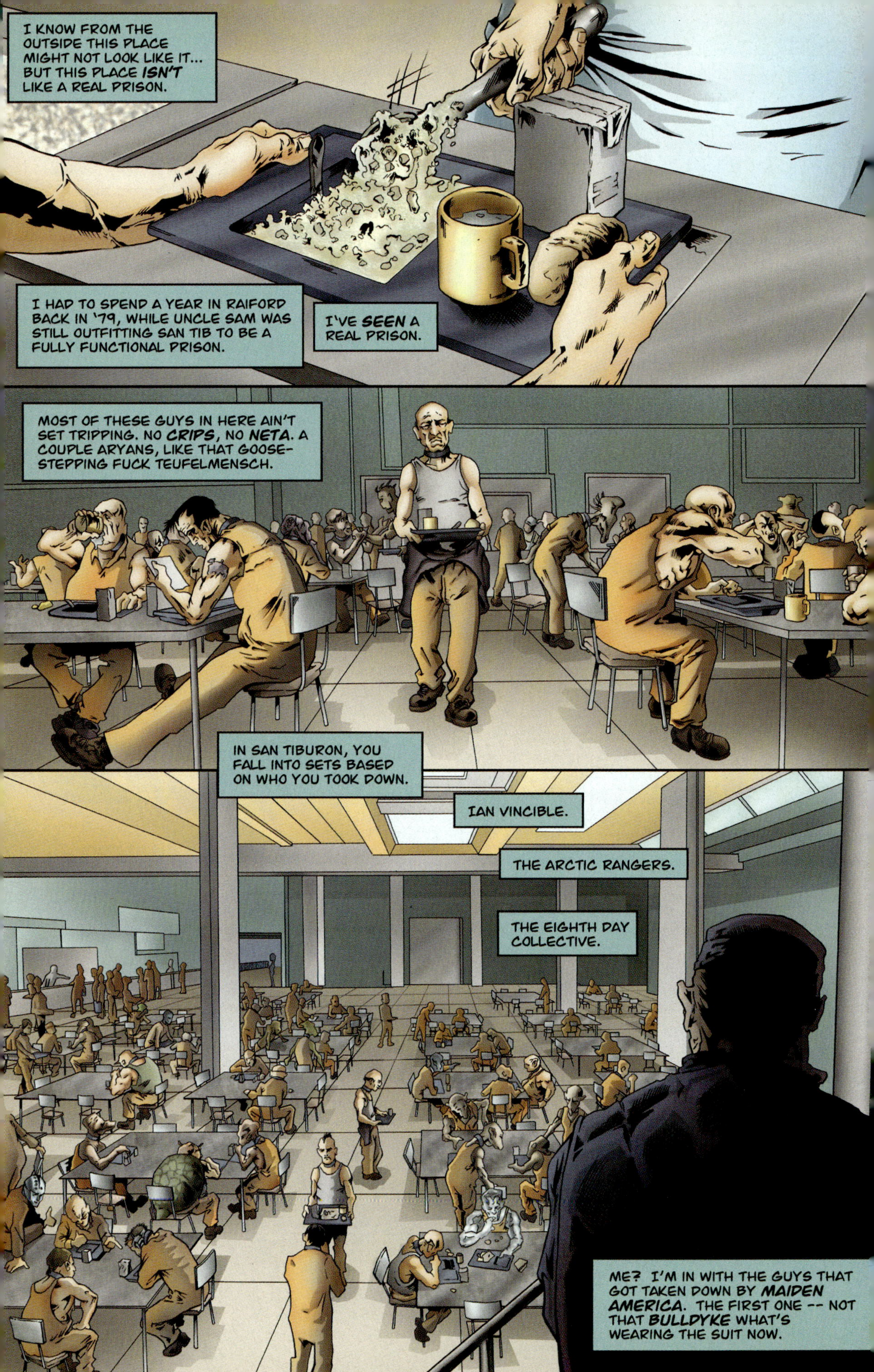
I KNOW FROM THE OUTSIDE THIS PLACE MIGHT NOT LOOK LIKE IT... BUT THIS PLACE ISN'T LIKE A REAL PRISON.
I HAD TO SPEND A YEAR IN RAIFORD BACK IN '79, WHILE UNCLE SAM WAS STILL OUTFITTING SAN TIB TO BE A FULLY FUNCTIONAL PRISON.
I'VE SEEN A REAL PRISON.
MOST OF THESE GUYS IN HERE AIN'T SET TRIPPING. NO CRIPS, NO NETA. A COUPLE ARYANS, LIKE THAT GOOSE-STEPPING FUCK TEUFELMENSCH.
IN SAN TIBURON, YOU FALL INTO SETS BASED ON WHO YOU TOOK DOWN.
IAN VINCIBLE.
THE ARCTIC RANGERS.
THE EIGHTH DAY COLLECTIVE.
ME? I'M IN WITH THE GUYS THAT GOT TAKEN DOWN BY MAIDEN AMERICA. THE FIRST ONE -- NOT THAT BULLDYKE WHAT'S WEARING THE SUIT NOW.

CANNOT BE. THAT IS UN-POSSIBLE.
ALL I KNOW'S WHAT I HEAR. AND I HEAR THAT NEW CAPTAIN'S A MEAN MOTHER FUCKER.
HEY, SHORT TIMER. PEOPLE ARE TALKING ABOUT THAT NEW C.O.
TOOFY SAID HE SAW HIM WALKING DOWN TO PAYBACK'S POD THE NIGHT BEFORE HE ENDED UP ALL FUCKED UP IN I.C.U.
TOOFY'S AN INBRED RACIST.
REGARDLESS, IT SERVES THAT BIBLE THUMPER RIGHT. I JUST WISH I COULD HAVE BEEN THERE WHEN HE GOT THE SHIT KICKED OUT OF HIM.
GRAVES, ISN'T YOUR POD NEXT DOOR?
YOU KNOW ME, BOYS. I KEEP MY MOUTH SHUT...
...I DIDN'T SEE SHIT.

ER... YEAH... I...
BESIDES, WHAT DOES IT MATTER?
IF BRODY ORDERED THE HIT, IT'S NO WORSE THAN WHAT THAT ASS-HOLE MAJORS DID BEFORE HIM.
EASY FOR YOU TO SAY. WE'RE ALL ON BUCK ROGERS TIME, OLD MAN. SKY'S GONNA BE FULL OF FLYING CARS 'AN SHIT BY THE TIME WE SEE DAYLIGHT.
NOT YOU, THOUGH. IN A COUPLE WEEKS, YOU'RE GONNA STEP UP TO THOSE GATES, AND BREATHE SWEET FREEDOM.
FIRST IT'S PAYBACK. MAYBE NEXT WEEK, IT'S TOOFY, OR GALLETINI. OR ONE OF US.
NOT THAT YOU HAVE TO CARE, GORDY. YOU'RE ALREADY GONE. DON'T NEED NO SPECIAL EYES TO SEE IT, EITHER.
FUCK YOU GUYS.

TWO HOURS LEFT.
ONLY 120 MINUTES UNTIL I CAN STATE, FOR THE RECORD, THAT 25 YEARS SPENT IN THIS PLACE HAVE TRANSFORMED ME INTO A MODEL CITIZEN.
D'YOU KNOW I WAS ONE OF THE FIRST ONES HERE?
THESE KIDS THAT CAME AFTER ME... I'M OLD ENOUGH TO BE MOST OF THEIR FATHERS.
I'M A 57 YEAR-OLD FORMER SUPERVILLAIN WITH A BAD HEART.
I TAKE MEDICATION FOR IT THAT PREVENTS ME, AMONG OTHER THINGS, FROM KEEPING AN ERECTION FOR LONGER THAN FOUR SECONDS.
I HAVE ARTHRITIS, BURSITIS, AND MY BLADDER'S NOT SO GOOD, EITHER.
YOU MAY BE SEATED, MISTER TWEEDY. THIS MEETING REGARDING THE PETITION FOR ELIGIBILITY OF PAROLE FOR PRISONER #T-10009 MAY NOW COME TO ORDER.
BUT I'M READY. I HAVE TESTIMONY FROM DOCTORS AND PSYCHOLOGISTS. I HAVE LEGAL PRECEDENTS. I HAVE CHARACTER WITNESS. CLASSES FOR COLLEGE CREDIT.
SHIT, I EVEN HAVE GOOD PERFORMANCE REPORT CARDS.

I STOOD THERE THAT DAY BEFORE THE PAROLE HEARING BOARD, AND TOLD 'EM THE REASONS THAT I SHOULD BE RELEASED.
SHOWED THEM ALL THE REASONS I WAS READY TO REJOIN POLITE SOCIETY.
AND THOSE SIX MEN AND WOMEN WERE *STUNNED*.
KNOCKED 'EM ON THEIR ASSES.
NEVER BEFORE HAD THEY HEARD SUCH A GOOD ARGUMENT FOR RELEASE.
BUT I SAW SOMETHING WHEN THEY LOOKED ME IN THE EYE THAT DAY...
...RIGHT BEFORE THEY *DENIED* MY PAROLE.
IT WAS A LOOK THAT TOLD ME I WAS KIDDIN' MYSELF.
THEY DIDN'T WANT ANY PART OF ME IN 'POLITE SOCIETY'.
I JUST DON'T KNOW WHO THE FUCK I WAS KIDDING. I WANTED TO SHOW THEM I WAS REFORMED. I WAS JUST LIKE THEM.
BUT WHAT I SAW IN THEIR EYES TOLD ME, I WASN'T LIKE THEM. I'D *NEVER* BE REFORMED.
I WAS A RATTLESNAKE WITHOUT FANGS. I WAS THAT *TIGER* THAT ATTACKED THOS TWO MAGICIAN FRUITS IN VEGAS.
AND THEY'D NEVER SEE ME ANY DIFFERENT. NOT IF I SERVED OUT A MILLION SENTENCES.

I KNEW IT THEN. AS CLEARLY AS I KNEW HOW MANY STEPS IT WAS DOWN THE STAIRS TO THE CAFETERIA.
THEY'D NEVER FORGIVE ME.
LIGHTS OUT! SHUT THE FUCK UP, LADIES!
POOOOOOMMMM
IT MADE ME CRAZY.
I'D DONE ALL I COULD DO... WHAT MORE DID THEY WANT FROM ME?
TWENTY-EIGHT YEARS I'D SPENT IN THIS PLACE. THEY OWED ME FOR THOSE YEARS.
AND I KNEW THEN WHAT I KNOW NOW... WHICH IS GORDON TWEEDY WAS GOING TO GO DOWN IN HISTORY AS THE FIRST MAN TO ESCAPE FROM SAN TIBURON.

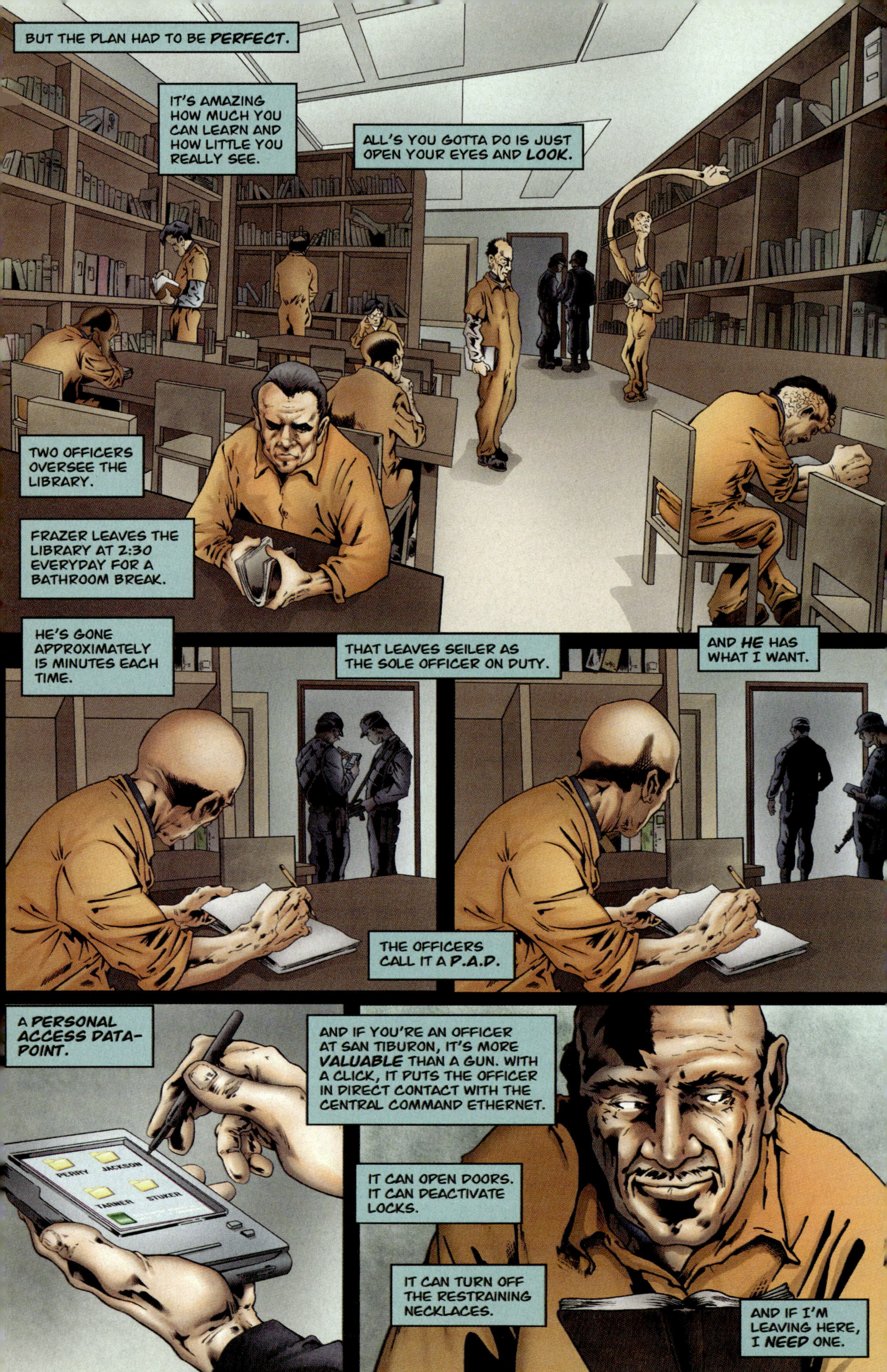
BUT THE PLAN HAD TO BE PERFECT.
IT'S AMAZING HOW MUCH YOU CAN LEARN AND HOW LITTLE YOU REALLY SEE.
ALL'S YOU GOTTA DO IS JUST OPEN YOUR EYES AND LOOK.
TWO OFFICERS OVERSEE THE LIBRARY.
FRAZER LEAVES THE LIBRARY AT 2:30 EVERYDAY FOR A BATHROOM BREAK.
HE'S GONE APPROXIMATELY 15 MINUTES EACH TIME.
THAT LEAVES SEILER AS THE SOLE OFFICER ON DUTY.
AND HE HAS WHAT I WANT.
THE OFFICERS CALL IT A P.A.D.
A PERSONAL ACCESS DATA-POINT.
AND IF YOU'RE AN OFFICER AT SAN TIBURON, IT'S MORE VALUABLE THAN A GUN. WITH A CLICK, IT PUTS THE OFFICER IN DIRECT CONTACT WITH THE CENTRAL COMMAND ETHERNET.
PERRY
JACKSON
TARNER
STUKER
IT CAN OPEN DOORS. IT CAN DEACTIVATE LOCKS.
IT CAN TURN OFF THE RESTRAINING NECKLACES.
AND IF I'M LEAVING HERE, I NEED ONE.

TWO WEEKS PASS AS I MAKE MY PLANS.

A BOOK FULL OF CODED NOTATIONS, DIAGRAMS, AND CHARTS ARE THE FRUIT OF MY LABOR.

A LOT OF SHIT NEEDS TO HAPPEN IN ORDER TO MAKE THIS WORK.

AT APPROXIMATELY 2:35, A FIGHT WILL BREAK OUT IN THE LIBRARY BETWEEN TWO INMATES. SINCE FRAZIER IS IN THE RESTROOM, SEILER WILL USE THE P.A.D. TO CALL IN A COLLAR SHOCK ON THEM BEFORE REQUESTING BACKUP FROM CENTRAL COMMAND..

A SENSOR ON THE NECKLACE'S HUD DISPLAY FLASHES RED A SECOND BEFORE THE ELETRICITY HITS.

TOO BAD MOST OFFICERS DON'T KNOW THAT... ESPECIALLY WHEN I SHOVE THE NECKLACE TOWARDS HIM.

IT'S NOT ENOUGH TO FRY HIM CRISPY, BUT IT'LL KNOCK HIM ON HIS ASS FOR A FEW MINUTES.

LONG ENOUGH TO GRAB THE GUYS P.A.D. AND MAKE A DASH FOR IT.

JUST GOTTA MAKE SURE TO ACTIVATE IT WITH THE OFFICER'S THUMBPRINT FIRST.

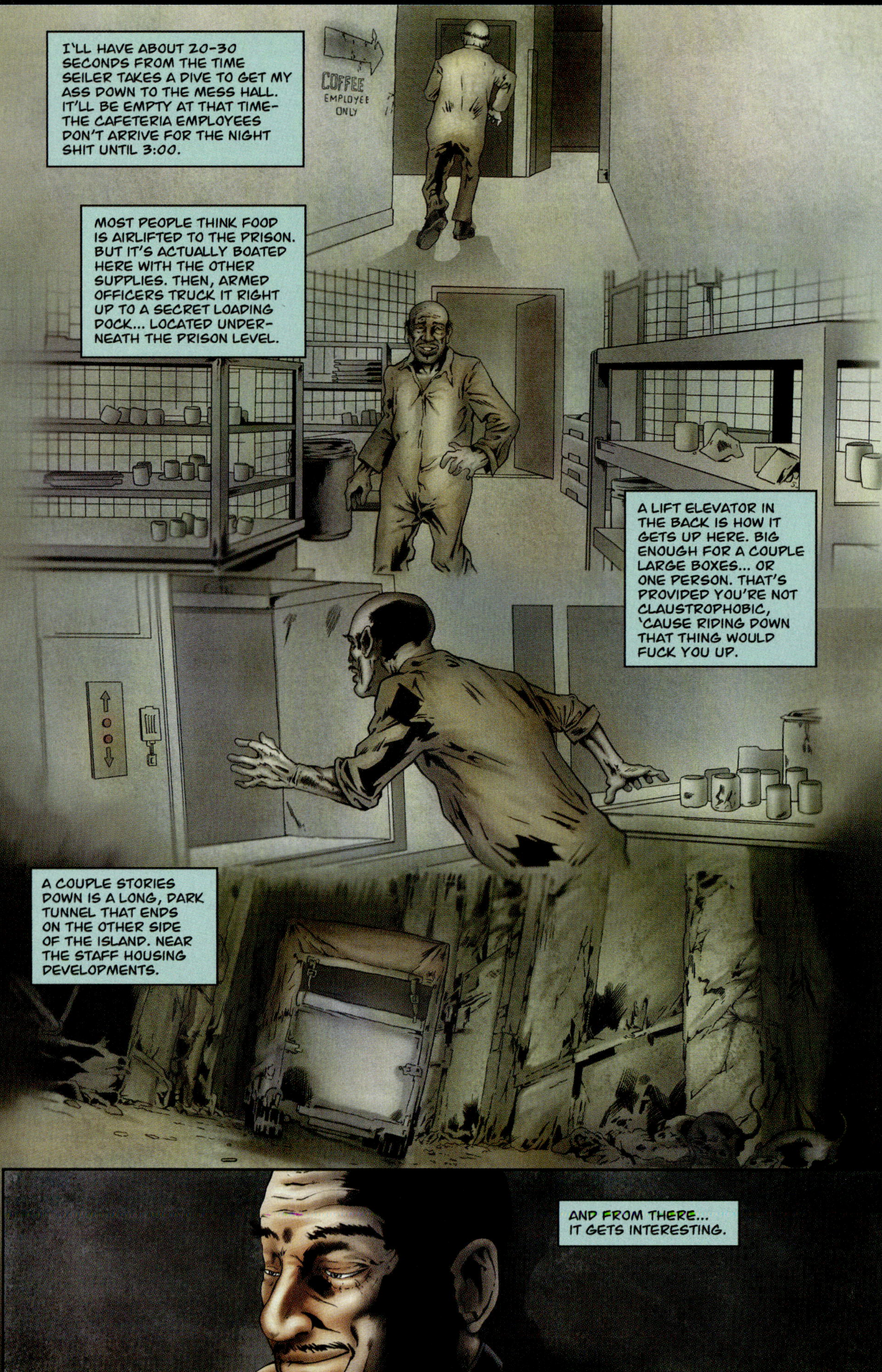
I'LL HAVE ABOUT 20-30 SECONDS FROM THE TIME SEILER TAKES A DIVE TO GET MY ASS DOWN TO THE MESS HALL. IT'LL BE EMPTY AT THAT TIME- THE CAFETERIA EMPLOYEES DON'T ARRIVE FOR THE NIGHT SHIT UNTIL 3:00.
COFFEE
EMPLOYEE ONLY
MOST PEOPLE THINK FOOD IS AIRLIFTED TO THE PRISON. BUT IT'S ACTUALLY BOATED HERE WITH THE OTHER SUPPLIES. THEN, ARMED OFFICERS TRUCK IT RIGHT UP TO A SECRET LOADING DOCK... LOCATED UNDER-NEATH THE PRISON LEVEL.
A LIFT ELEVATOR IN THE BACK IS HOW IT GETS UP HERE. BIG ENOUGH FOR A COUPLE LARGE BOXES... OR ONE PERSON. THAT'S PROVIDED YOU'RE NOT CLAUSTROPHOBIC, 'CAUSE RIDING DOWN THAT THING WOULD FUCK YOU UP.
A COUPLE STORIES DOWN IS A LONG, DARK TUNNEL THAT ENDS ON THE OTHER SIDE OF THE ISLAND. NEAR THE STAFF HOUSING DEVELOPMENTS.
AND FROM THERE... IT GETS INTERESTING.

...SO HERE'S HOPING NOBODY GETS IN MY WAY.
HEY THERE. THE KIDS BEING GOOD TODAY?
COUPLE ELBOWS THROWN IN THAT PICKUP GAME. OTHERWISE, IT'S SMOOTH SAILING.
I HAVEN'T HAD A CHANCE TO INTRODUCE MYSELF TO EVERY-BODY YET. I'M--
HOLD THAT THOUGHT JUST A SECOND, CAPTAIN.
TOOMEY! DROP THE GRUDGE AND PUT DOWN THE BARBELL, OR SO HELP ME GOD I'LL JOLT YOU UNTIL LOCKDOWN TONIGHT! DON'T MAKE ME COME OVER THERE!
OH, FOR THE LOVE OF... HOLD ON A SECOND.
WHAT DID I TELL YOU, HUH?
BZZZTT
TOUGH CASE?
TOUGHER ON HIM THAN ME.
I CAN SEE THAT.
CAPTAIN JASON BRODY.
OFFICER LIZ MORALES.
FEEL LIKE CATCHING THE NEW GUY UP ON THE LOCAL GOSSIP?

UH, SURE. WITH ALL DUE RESPECT SIR, WHY ASK ME?
THE PERSONNEL FILES SHOULD BE AVAILABLE ON YOUR P.A.D.
I'VE READ THE FILES.
WHAT I DON'T GET FROM THEM IS THE WAY THESE GUYS INTERACT WITH EACH OTHER WHEN THEY THINK WE'RE NOT WATCHING.
RELATIONSHIPS, MOTIVATIONS... WHO'S DOING THE FUCKING AND WHO'S GETTING FUCKED.
PARDON THE LANGUAGE, OFFICER.
NO FUCKING PROBLEM.
CAPTAIN.
LIKE HIM. THE BIG GUY WITH THE SWASTIKA. WHAT'S HIS DEAL?
THAT'S HENDRIK NEINHARDT. HE GOES BY ***TEUFELMENSCH***, LITERALLY DEVIL MAN.
CUTE. HE GETS A WIDE BERTH AROUND HERE. THAT INTENTIONAL?
NO QUESTION. TOOFEY'S THE ***ALPHA MALE*** HERE IN V.C. EVERYBODY'S AFRAID OF HIM, EVEN SOME OF THE PRISON STAFF.
DR. JOSEPHS WON'T EVEN TREAT HIM ANYMORE. AFTER HE SNAPPED OFF AN ORDERLY'S FINGER DURING IMMUNIZATION WEEK.
JESUS.
BUT IF YOU THINK HE LOOKS STRONG NOW, IT'S ***NOTHING*** COMPARED TO WHAT HE'D BE LIKE WITH-OUT ONE.
I'VE SEEN HIM THROW CARS AROUND LIKE PAPER AIRPLANES.
GUYS WITH NO FRIENDS USUALLY MAKE UP FOR IT BY HAVING PLENTY OF ENEMIES.

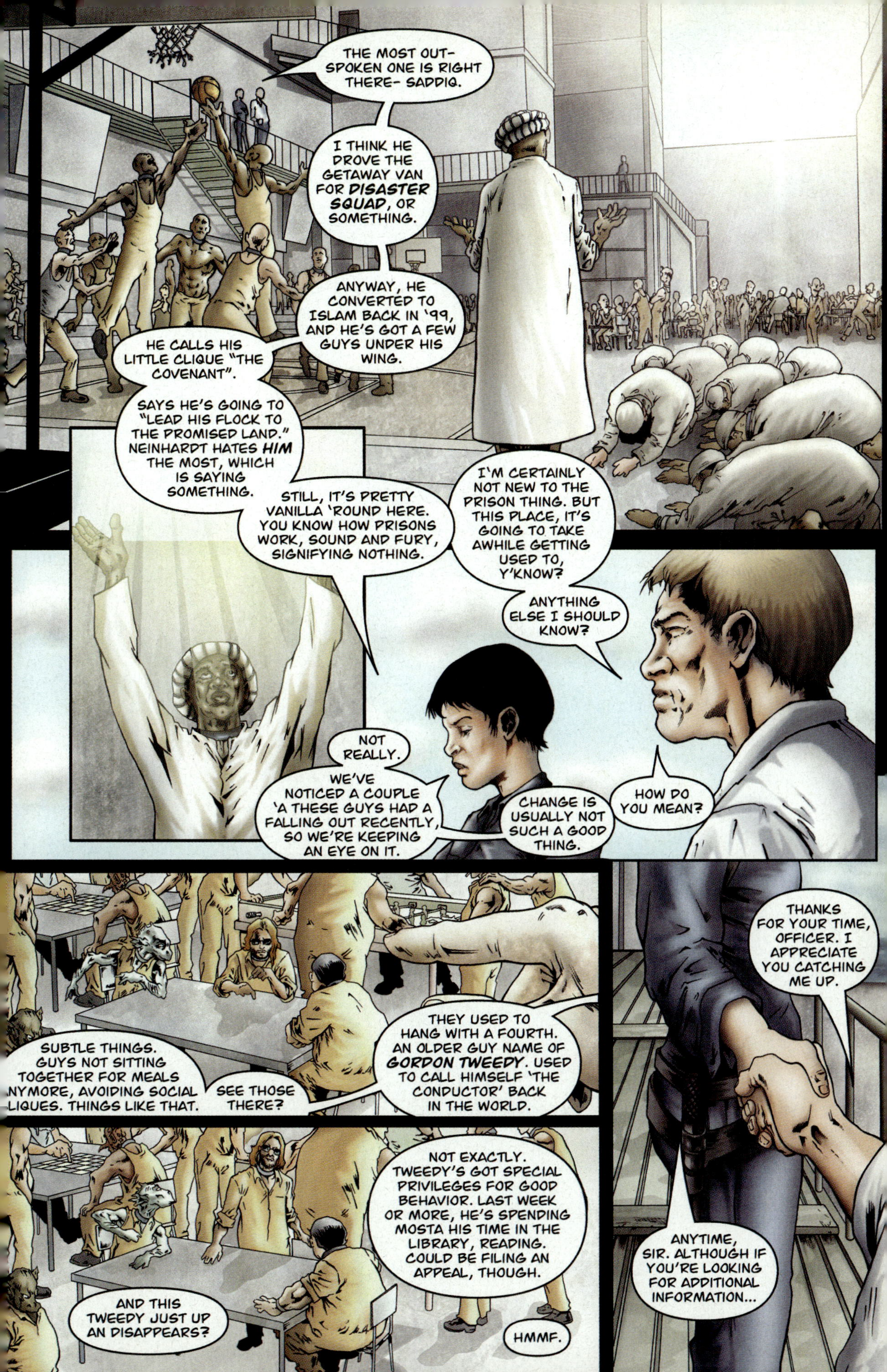
THE MOST OUT-SPOKEN ONE IS RIGHT THERE- SADDIQ.
I THINK HE DROVE THE GETAWAY VAN FOR **DISASTER SQUAD**, OR SOMETHING.
ANYWAY, HE CONVERTED TO ISLAM BACK IN '99, AND HE'S GOT A FEW GUYS UNDER HIS WING.
HE CALLS HIS LITTLE CLIQUE "THE COVENANT".
SAYS HE'S GOING TO "LEAD HIS FLOCK TO THE PROMISED LAND." NEINHARDT HATES **HIM** THE MOST, WHICH IS SAYING SOMETHING.
STILL, IT'S PRETTY VANILLA 'ROUND HERE. YOU KNOW HOW PRISONS WORK, SOUND AND FURY, SIGNIFYING NOTHING.
I'M CERTAINLY NOT NEW TO THE PRISON THING. BUT THIS PLACE, IT'S GOING TO TAKE AWHILE GETTING USED TO, Y'KNOW?
ANYTHING ELSE I SHOULD KNOW?
NOT REALLY.
WE'VE NOTICED A COUPLE 'A THESE GUYS HAD A FALLING OUT RECENTLY, SO WE'RE KEEPING AN EYE ON IT.
CHANGE IS USUALLY NOT SUCH A GOOD THING.
HOW DO YOU MEAN?
SUBTLE THINGS. GUYS NOT SITTING TOGETHER FOR MEALS NYMORE, AVOIDING SOCIAL LIQUES. THINGS LIKE THAT.
SEE THOSE THERE?
THEY USED TO HANG WITH A FOURTH. AN OLDER GUY NAME OF **GORDON TWEEDY**. USED TO CALL HIMSELF 'THE CONDUCTOR' BACK IN THE WORLD.
AND THIS TWEEDY JUST UP AN DISAPPEARS?
NOT EXACTLY. TWEEDY'S GOT SPECIAL PRIVILEGES FOR GOOD BEHAVIOR. LAST WEEK OR MORE, HE'S SPENDING MOSTA HIS TIME IN THE LIBRARY, READING. COULD BE FILING AN APPEAL, THOUGH.
HMMF.
THANKS FOR YOUR TIME, OFFICER. I APPRECIATE YOU CATCHING ME UP.
ANYTIME, SIR. ALTHOUGH IF YOU'RE LOOKING FOR ADDITIONAL INFORMATION...

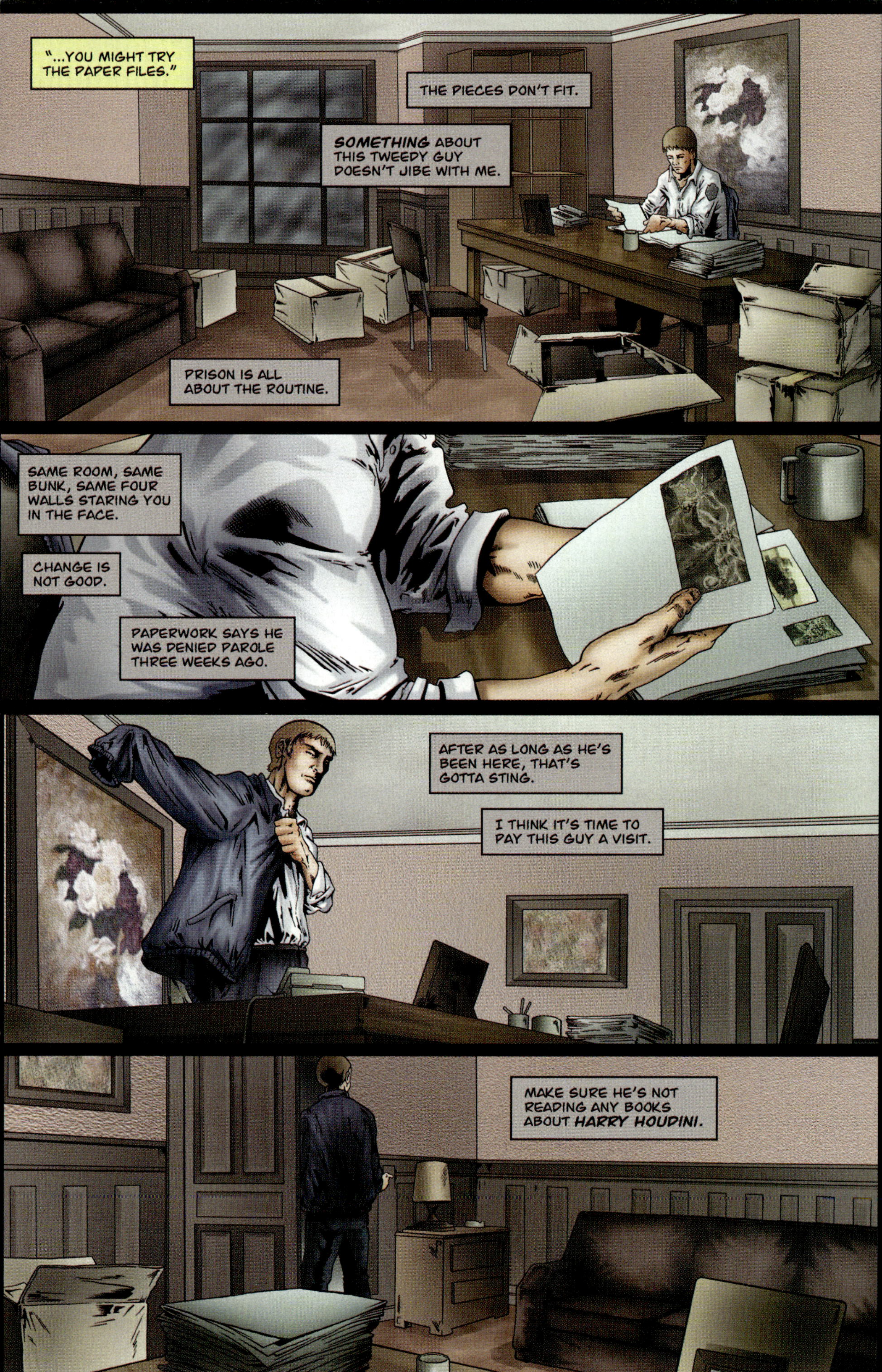
"...YOU MIGHT TRY THE PAPER FILES."
THE PIECES DON'T FIT.
SOMETHING ABOUT THIS TWEEDY GUY DOESN'T JIBE WITH ME.
PRISON IS ALL ABOUT THE ROUTINE.
SAME ROOM, SAME BUNK, SAME FOUR WALLS STARING YOU IN THE FACE.
CHANGE IS NOT GOOD.
PAPERWORK SAYS HE WAS DENIED PAROLE THREE WEEKS AGO.
AFTER AS LONG AS HE'S BEEN HERE, THAT'S GOTTA STING.
I THINK IT'S TIME TO PAY THIS GUY A VISIT.
MAKE SURE HE'S NOT READING ANY BOOKS ABOUT HARRY HOUDINI.

MY THROAT IS DRY AND MY HANDS ARE SHAKING.
BUT IF IT'S GOING TO HAPPEN, IT NEEDS TO HAPPEN **NOW**.

SO, I WALK OVER TO DERON, AND WHISPER THE WORDS I **KNOW** WILL START THE CHAIN OF DOMINOS.
"HOLLOWAY SAID HE'S SURPRISED YOU ALABAMA NIGGERS CAN READ BOOKS WITH NO PICTURES IN 'EM."

UHN?

KRAK!

HOLLOWAY KILL YOU, MUD MAN!

GUYS, GUYS! SETTLE DOWN! COME ON NOW!

GOTTA TIME THIS JUST RIGHT...

OH FU--

AAARRGH!

AAARRGH!

AAARRGH!

STUPID, STUPID, STUPID.
I'M IN THE WORST POSITION OF MY LIFE, AND ALL I CAN THINK ABOUT IS THAT STUPID KID IN THAT NEWS CLIPPING.
YOU KNOW, THE ONE I DON'T HAVE ANYTHING IN COMMON WITH ANYMORE.
I'M THINKING ABOUT HOW FAR I'VE COME IN 28 YEARS. HOW MUCH I'VE REFORMED.
CURRENTLY IN PURSUIT OF PRISONER TWEEDY, GORDON A.
PRISONER IS WITHOUT HIS RESTRAINT.
REQUEST IMMEDIATE LOCKDOWN FOR VIOLENT CRIME WING UNTIL ALL CLEAR.
TWEEDY! STOP! DON'T DO THIS!

THAT KID IN THE PHOTOGRAPH, HE KILLED PEOPLE FOR NOTHING MORE THAN DEAD PRESIDENTS ON GREEN PAPER.
GORDON! NOBODY'S GOING TO HURT YOU, JUST COME OUT AND WE'LL TALK... OKAY?
TODAY, IT'LL BE DIFFERENT.
GORDON...?
TODAY, I KILL TO EARN MY FREEDOM.

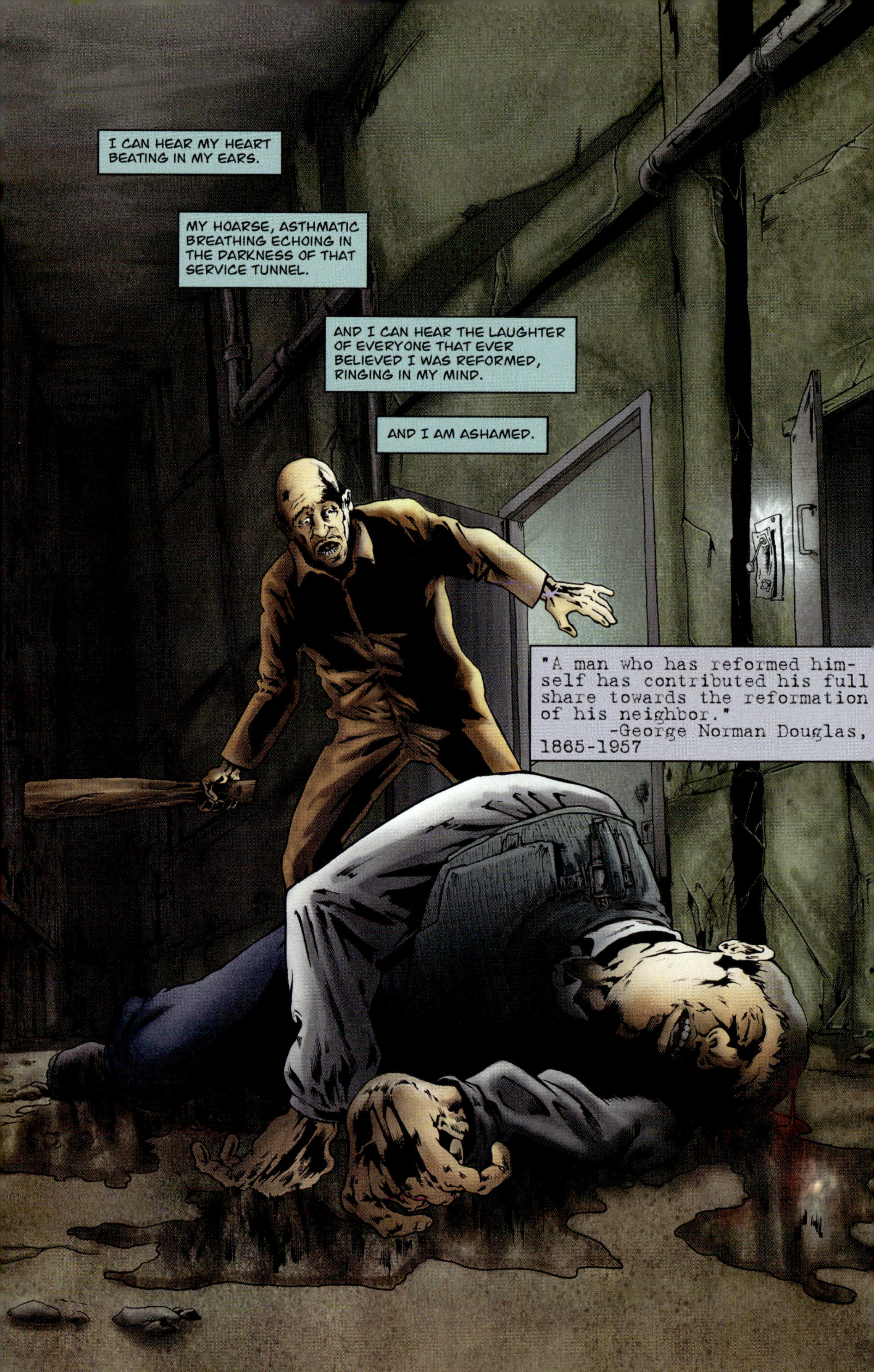
I CAN HEAR MY HEART BEATING IN MY EARS.
MY HOARSE, ASTHMATIC BREATHING ECHOING IN THE DARKNESS OF THAT SERVICE TUNNEL.
AND I CAN HEAR THE LAUGHTER OF EVERYONE THAT EVER BELIEVED I WAS REFORMED, RINGING IN MY MIND.
AND I AM ASHAMED.
"A man who has reformed himself has contributed his full share towards the reformation of his neighbor." -George Norman Douglas, 1865-1957

CHAPTER 5

CORRECTIVE
MEASURES
53-7271

I'M SECONDS AWAY FROM KILLING THIS MAN IN COLD BLOOD WHEN THE MEMORY HITS ME...
MY FAMILY DIDN'T HAVE MUCH MONEY GROWING UP.
TO PASS THE TIME, MY BROTHER RAY AND I USED TO SET UP ROWS OF DOMINOS THROUGH THE HOUSE.
WE'D TRY AND SEE HOW MANY WE COULD GET TO FALL ALL IN A ROW.
WHEN WE PLANNED IT OUT RIGHT, IT'D ALL COME DOWN JUST THE WAY IT WAS SUPPOSED TO...
...ONE BY ONE.
AND WHEN IT DIDN'T, THE DOMINOS WOULD JUST...
...STOP.
THUNK

SPLISH
SORRY CAP, BUT I'M GONNA NEED THIS MORE THAN YOU.
YOU UNDER-STAND...

STORY * PENCILS * COLORS * LETTERS
Grant Chastain * Fran Moyano * Jay Moyano * Mike Storniolo
DOMINOES
COPY SIX-TWO-ONE
BE ADVISED, LOCKDOWN CODE ECHO-FIVE ON ALL ISLAND TRANSPORTATION.
BLACKHAWK'S IN THE AIR, ASSISTANT WARDEN.
AERIAL THERMAL IMAGING IS TRAINED ON THE EXITS AROUND THE TUNNEL, AND THE MOTION SENSOR GRID HAS BEEN ARMED.
UN-FUCKING-BELIEVEABLE.
BE ADVISED BRAVO AND CHARLIE TEAMS ARE EN-ROUTE. SALLY-PORT DOORS ARE LOCKED DOWN AND SECURE.
THIS'LL ALL BE OVER SHORTLY, SIR.
EVERYTHING BUT THE FUCKING PAPERWORK...

COM-SAT
LINK
REQUESTED
UH... SIR...
THERE'S AN EMERGENCY CALL FROM THE... ER, WARDEN DEVLIN. SHOULD I UH--
NO... OFFICER, HE ALREADY KNOWS.
BUT SIR, HOW COULD HE ALR--
PATCH IT THROUGH TO MY PAD.
I'LL EXPECT GOOD NEWS WHEN I RETURN.
WELL, HEL-LO THERE, ROLAND!
AND HOW'S EVERY LITTLE THING BACK HOME?

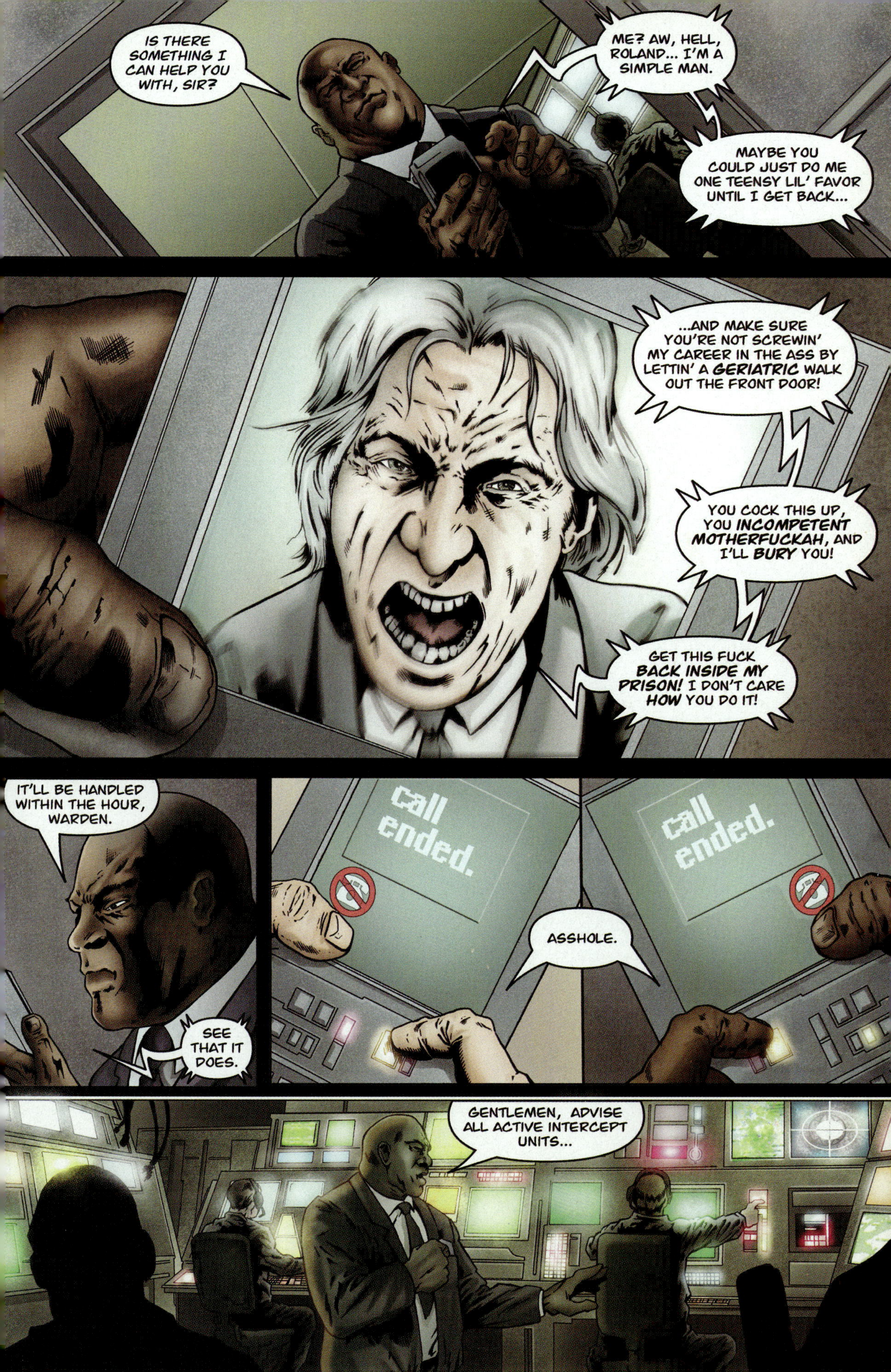
IS THERE SOMETHING I CAN HELP YOU WITH, SIR?
ME? AW, HELL, ROLAND... I'M A SIMPLE MAN.
MAYBE YOU COULD JUST DO ME ONE TEENSY LIL' FAVOR UNTIL I GET BACK...
...AND MAKE SURE YOU'RE NOT SCREWIN' MY CAREER IN THE ASS BY LETTIN' A GERIATRIC WALK OUT THE FRONT DOOR!
YOU COCK THIS UP, YOU INCOMPETENT MOTHERFUCKAH, AND I'LL BURY YOU!
GET THIS FUCK BACK INSIDE MY PRISON! I DON'T CARE HOW YOU DO IT!
IT'LL BE HANDLED WITHIN THE HOUR, WARDEN.
SEE THAT IT DOES.
call ended.
call ended.
ASSHOLE.
GENTLEMEN, ADVISE ALL ACTIVE INTERCEPT UNITS...

"...GORDON TWEEDY'S TO BE TAKEN IN *ALIVE*."

HUFF

WHUFF

HUFF

BY MY ORIGINAL CALCULATIONS, THE SERVICE TUNNEL IS A HALF-MILE OF POORLY-LIT, BADLY-MAINTAINED *UP HILL SHIT*.

THERE'S *ONE* EXIT - A SALLYPORT DOOR THAT OPENS ONTO A DIRT ROAD THROUGH THE JUNGLE.

CNTRL, WHVAM-DWN... SRYUOKY, WHPND?
UNGGGHHHH....
NUH SGNOFTWDY, CNTRL, ECHOTM NFULPRSUIT... SIR, CNYUSTRD?
MMOKAY.
SNEAKY LIL' BASTARD CRACKED ME INNA HEAD'A GOOD ONE, THOUGH.
MEDICAL TEAM SHOULD BE DOWN HERE SHORTLY, SIR.
IN THE MEANTIME, SIT TIGHT. WE'RE MOVING TO INTERCEPT.
I'M CUH-COMING.
NEGATIVE, CAPTAIN. YOU AREN'T IN ANY CONDI--
FFPPPP
LEAD. THE. FUCKING. WAY.

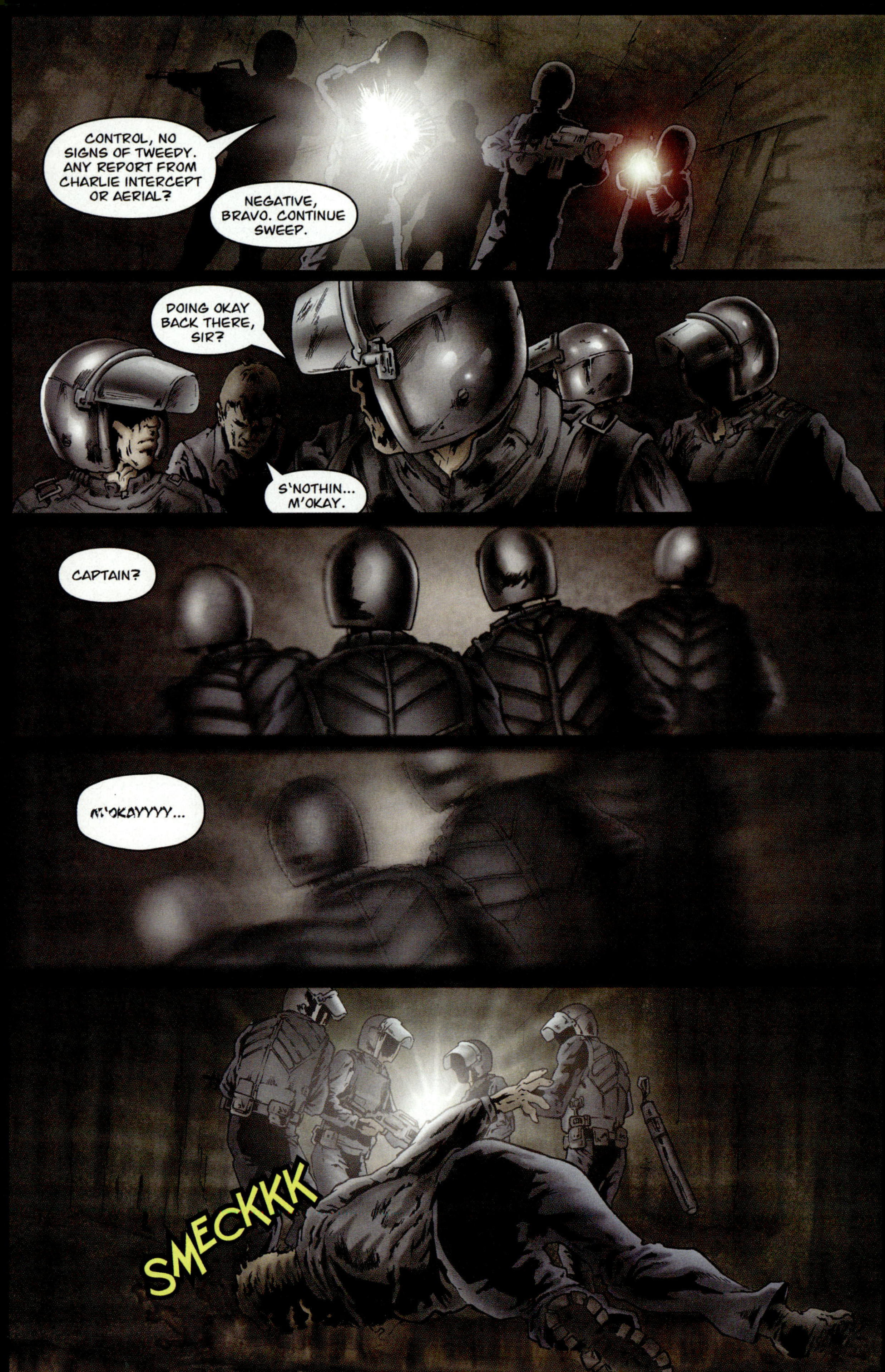
CONTROL, NO SIGNS OF TWEEDY. ANY REPORT FROM CHARLIE INTERCEPT OR AERIAL?
NEGATIVE, BRAVO. CONTINUE SWEEP.
DOING OKAY BACK THERE, SIR?
S'NOTHIN... M'OKAY.
CAPTAIN?
M'OKAYYYY...
SMECKKK

THIS ***BITCH***,
FOR EXAMPLE.
OFFICER MORALES.

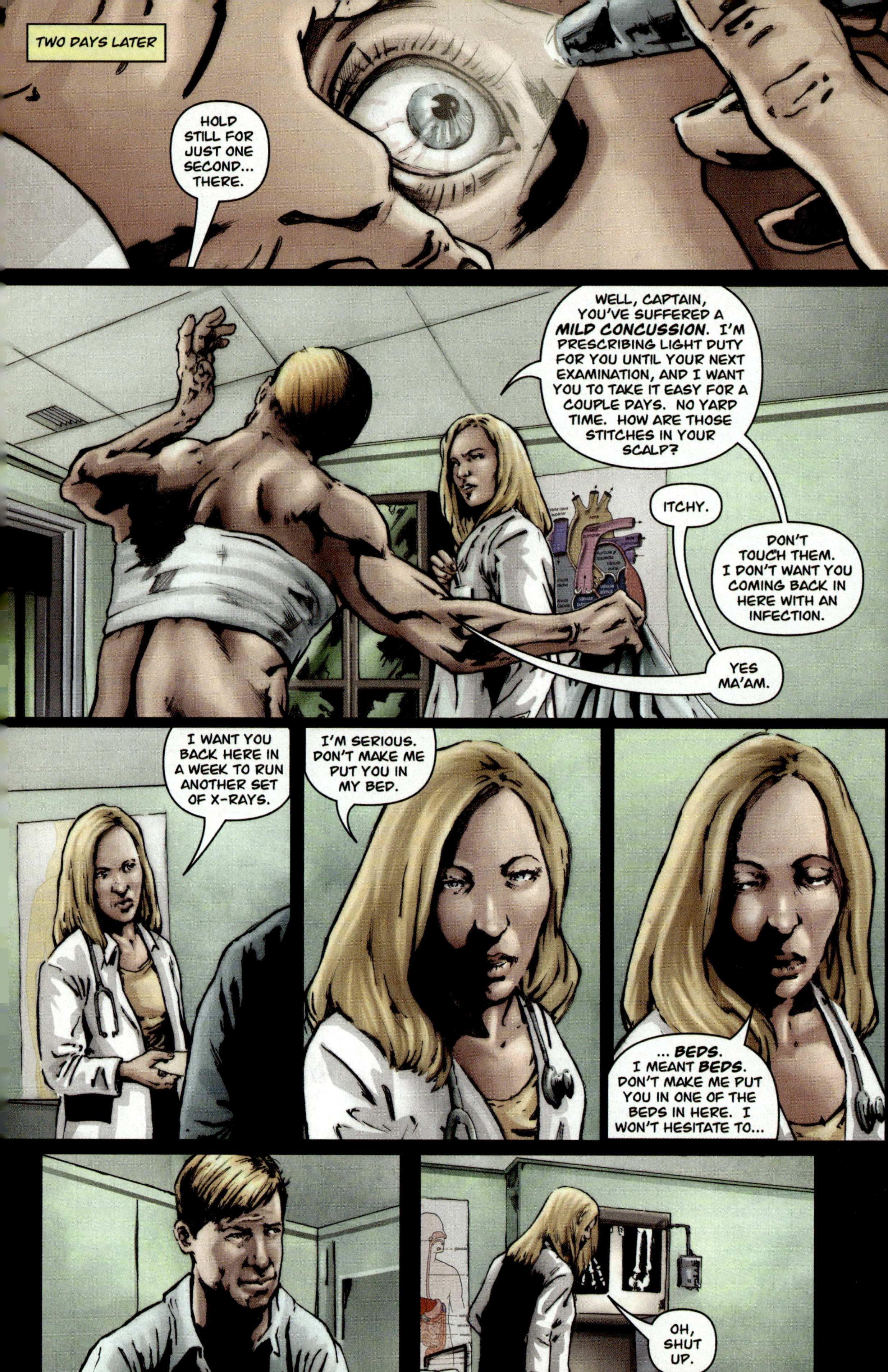
TWO DAYS LATER
HOLD STILL FOR JUST ONE SECOND... THERE.
WELL, CAPTAIN, YOU'VE SUFFERED A MILD CONCUSSION. I'M PRESCRIBING LIGHT DUTY FOR YOU UNTIL YOUR NEXT EXAMINATION, AND I WANT YOU TO TAKE IT EASY FOR A COUPLE DAYS. NO YARD TIME. HOW ARE THOSE STITCHES IN YOUR SCALP?
ITCHY.
DON'T TOUCH THEM. I DON'T WANT YOU COMING BACK IN HERE WITH AN INFECTION.
YES MA'AM.
I WANT YOU BACK HERE IN A WEEK TO RUN ANOTHER SET OF X-RAYS.
I'M SERIOUS. DON'T MAKE ME PUT YOU IN MY BED.
... BEDS. I MEANT BEDS. DON'T MAKE ME PUT YOU IN ONE OF THE BEDS IN HERE. I WON'T HESITATE TO...
OH, SHUT UP.

THANKS FOR THE QUICK ONCE-OVER, DOC.
IT'S THE LEAST I CAN DO FOR THE OTHER DAY.
I SHOULDN'T HAVE GONE OFF ON YOU LIKE I DID.
HOW IS WALTER LOCKE DOING THESE DAYS?
SO FAR HE'S UNRESPONSIVE.
THERE'S NO BRAIN TRAUMA ACCORDING TO THE CT SCAN. HIS BODY'S HEALING AT AN AMAZING RATE... HE'S JUST NOT COMING OUT OF THE COMA.
I'M ASSUMING I DON'T NEED TO ASK THAT I BE NOTIFIED IMMEDIATELY IF THAT CONDITION CHANGES.
AND I ASSUME YOU'LL CONTACT ME IF YOU NEED MEDICAL ATTENTION.
...YOU KNOW, YOU JUST WANT TO TALK, OR... RAB A BEER OR SOMETHING.
UH... WELL, I...
CAPTAIN BRODY?

"... THE ASSISTANT WARDEN WANTS TO SEE YOU IN HIS OFFICE IMMEDIATELY."
YOU'RE QUITE THE INTERESTING MAN, BRODY. I'M AFRAID I DIDN'T KNOW YOUR PEDIGREE WHEN I MET YOU A COUPLE WEEKS AGO.
PURPLE HEART... SILVER STAR...
YOU'RE JUST A REGULAR JOE HERO.
SIR, IF THIS IS ABOUT THE TWEEDY INCIDENT...
CAPTAIN, DO YOU KNOW WHERE THE TERM "LOOSE CANNON" CAME FROM?
SEE, IT COMES FROM OLD SEA MERCHANTS. KIND OF GUYS THAT USED TO SHIP NIGGERS FROM AFRICA TO THE "LAND OF THE FREE". IF YOU HAD A "LOOSE CANNON" ON DECK... YOU NEVER KNEW WHAT MIGHT HAPPEN.
MAYBE IT FALLS OVERBOARD. MAYBE IT ROLLS OVER SOMEBODY. OR MAYBE IT GOES OFF, PUTTING A STEEL BALL THROUGH SOMEBODY'S HEAD.

LET'S IGNORE FOR A MOMENT YOUR... AHEM, "RECENT SPOTTY WORK HISTORY", CAPTAIN. LET'S FOCUS INSTEAD ON HOW YOU CAN BEST BECOME A TEAM PLAYER AROUND HERE.
THERE'S BEEN A BIT OF A SITUATION INVOLVING A COUPLE OF OUR RESIDENTS HERE AT SAN TIBURON. SOME CONSIDERABLE RACIAL STATIC.
THE PRISON'S EXPECTING SOME HIGH-PROFILE VISITORS THIS WEEK. THESE VISITORS NEED TO BE IMPRESSED WITH HOW WELL SAN TIBURON IS RUN.
BRAIN-JOLT. SOLITARY CONFINEMENT.
NOT AN OPTION THIS TIME.
DO YOU MIND IF I ASK WHY NOT?
ONLY IF YOU DON'T MIND WHEN I TELL YOU IT'S NONE OF YOUR GODDAMN BUSINESS.
HMMMM. NEINHARDT AND SADDIQ.
YOU KNOW THEM?
MORALES CLUED ME IN ON THEM A COUPLE DAYS AGO. SAID THERE'S A LOT OF BAD BLOOD THERE.

CAPTAIN, I'M LEAVING IT UP TO YOU TO DECIDE HOW THIS SITUATION IS RESOLVED... SO LONG AS THE TWO OF THEM REMAIN BENEATH THE RADAR OF OUR VISITORS.
PERHAPS I SHOULD WARN YOU WE'RE BEING AUDITED BY THE BUREAU OF PRISONS. SO DEALING WITH THEM IN THE SAME MANNER AS YOU DEALT WITH WALTER LOCKE MIGHT NOT BE IN YOUR BEST INTERESTS.
I TRUST THIS REQUIRES NO FURTHER EXPOSITION?
...NO SIR.
GOOD. WHEN YOU'RE FINISHED, SAN TIBURON POLICY HAS A SUGGESTED THREE-DAY MEDICAL LEAVE FOR ALL ASSAULTED PERSONNEL.
I ADVISE YOU TO TAKE IT.

WHASSUP, NEW BOSS?
WHOOOO-WEEEE! BACON ON THE PROWL!
PART WATERS, MY BROTHERS...
... AND ALLOW THIS MAN PASSAGE INTO MY KINGDOM.
GENTLEMEN, LEAVE US - WE SHALL CONGREGATE TOMORROW FOR PRAYER.
HOW CAN THE MUSLIM COVENANT HELP YOU, JASON BRODY?
TELL ME ABOUT NEINHARDT, SADDIQ. I NEED TO KNOW WHAT'S GOING ON BETWEEN YOU TWO.

NEINHARDT IS A FOUL-MOUTHED SUPREMACIST. WHEN LAST I SPOKE WITH HIM, HE THREATENED TO REMOVE MY HEAD AND DEFECATE IN THE RESULTANT CAVITY.
MY PEOPLE KEEP AN ACTIVE EYE ON HIM AND HIS "WHITE POWER" LUNACY.
ANY CHANCE "YOUR PEOPLE" MIGHT BE PLOTTING SOMETHING AGAINST NEINHARDT?
MALCOLM
WE ARE MEN OF ALLAH, CAPTAIN. WE CONCERN OURSELVES ONLY WITH SUPPLICATION IN THE EYES OF GOD.
THOUGH I SCARCELY EXPECT A MAN SUCH AS YOU TO KNOW ANYTHING OF SPIRITUAL PEACE.
FUNNY, YOUR FILE DOESN'T INDICATE YOU WERE VERY INTERESTED IN 'SPIRITUAL PEACE' WHEN YOU SHOT THOSE THREE BANK OFFICERS IN ENGLEWOOD.
VIOLENCE HAS NO FOOTHOLD IN MY HEART ANY LONGER, CAPTAIN.
TELL ME... CAN YOU SAY THE SAME?

THIS IS THE ONLY NOTICE YOU GET, SADDIQ. STAY AWAY FROM NEINHARDT.
HA HA HA! AS-SALLAMU ALEYKUM, CAPTAIN... PEACE BE UNTO YOU THIS DAY!
BITCH NEEDS AN ATTITUDE ADJUSTMENT, YOU ASK ME.
CALM, MY HOLY BROTHERS... WHEN THE MOMENT IS RIGHT...
... WE MAY BE ABLE TO RID OURSELVES OF TWO PROBLEMS AT ONCE.

...BALD FLATTERN HITLER-FAHNEN UBER ALLEN STRASSEN, DIE KNECHTSCHAFT DAUERT NUR MEHR KURZE ZEIT...
NEINHARDT.
...SAME DIE FAHNE HOCK DIE REIHEN FEST GESCHLOSSEN, S.A. MARSCHIERT MIT RUHIG FESTUM SCHRITT...
NEINHARDT.
LET'S HAVE A LITTLE TALK.

HANDS BEHIND YOUR BACK, HENDRIK.
MOVING A LITTLE QUICKLY, AREN'T YOU, CAPTAIN? YOU HAVEN'T EVEN TAKEN ME OUT TO DINNER YET.
YOU AND I ARE JUST GOING TO TAKE A LITTLE TRIP DOWN THE HALL, AND HAVE A LITTLE CHAT ABOUT EQUALITY.

NICE AND EASY, HENDRIK.

CAPTAIN! BEHIND YOU!

WHIZZZZ
MUH-FUCKA!

THWAP

UNGGGGH!!
CRUNCHHHH

WHAT THE FUCK!
ALLAHU AKBAR! DEATH TO THE WHITE DEVIL, AND ANY THAT ABIDE HIS HATRED!

RIP HIS HEAD OFF, BRODY! SHOW ZEM ZAT THE TRIUMPH OF THE WILL IS MIGHTY AND SURE!

SHUT THE FUCK UP, NEINHARDT!
MORALES... I NEED YOU FRONT AND CENTER.
SIR.
TAKE THE SHITBAG WITH THE BROKEN TEETH TO THE INFIRMARY, AND THEN PUT HIM IN ISOLATION. SIX WEEKS WITH NO CONTACT TO GEN POP.
YES SIR. WHAT ABOUT NEINHARDT?
TAKE HIM AND SADDIQ TO INTERROGATION ROOM FOUR. I'LL BE DOWN THERE IN ABOUT AN HOUR.
I'M PUTTING A STOP TO THIS SHIT ONCE AND FOR ALL.

I ASSUME THIS IS *YOUR* DOING, **REDNECK**.

JUST WAIT UNTIL I CAN GET MY HANDS AROUND *YOUR* NECK. IT WILL BE A PLEASURE TO WATCH YOUR EYES POP OUT OF YOUR SKULL, NIGGER.

THANK YOU FOR THE ASSISTANCE, OFFICER MORALES. I CAN HANDLE IT FROM HERE.

I'LL BE HONEST WITH YOU TWO – I'VE DONE SOME THINGS IN MY LIFE THAT I'M ASHAMED OF.
I HAVEN'T ALWAYS BEEN FAIR, AND I HAVEN'T ALWAYS TREATED PEOPLE AS EQUALS.
I HAVEN'T ALWAYS TOLD THE TRUTH, EITHER.
ESPECIALLY WHEN I FELT IT SERVED THE GREATER GOOD NOT TO.

SCHWEINEHUND!
YOU THINK THE WHITE MAN'S LIES ARE ANYTHING NEW TO THE SONS OF ALLAH? MY PEOPLE...
SHUT THE FUCK UP. IT DOESN'T MATTER WHETHER YOUR PEOPLE BELIEVE THEY'RE TRUE...
... BECAUSE HIS PEOPLE WILL.
THE WAY I SEE IT, THAT PAINTS A WHOLE NEW TARGET ON EACH OF YOUR BACKS.
AND WHO DO YOU THINK THEY'LL TURN ON NEXT?
IF YOU CAN'T GO ANOTHER DAY WITHOUT HATING SOMEBODY, THEN FIND A MIRROR.
BECAUSE THE WAY I SEE IT, BOTH OF YOU RACIST ASSHOLES OWE A LOT MORE OF YOUR PROBLEMS TO YOURSELVES THAN ANYBODY ELSE.
OFFICERS WILL BE ALONG SHORTLY TO TUCK YOU BOTH IN FOR THE NIGHT. YOU'RE BOTH ON LOCKDOWN FOR THE NEXT SEVEN DAYS.
OH, AND FOR THE RECORD... THE FRIEND OF MINE THAT HELPED ME WITH THE PHOTOS IS NAMED KLEIN. AND HE DIDN'T CHARGE ME A DIME SO LONG AS I GAVE YOU BOTH A LITTLE MESSAGE:

"KISS MY WHITE JEWISH ASS."
EVERYTHING OKAY IN THERE?
SHOULD BE NOW. ASK OFFICERS GEEN AND VASQUEZ TO ESCORT THEM BOTH BACK TO THE ISOLATION PODS. I WANT THEM COOLING THEIR HEELS UNTIL FURTHER NOTICE.
THAT'S TWO ASSAULTS IN TWO DAYS FOR YOU.
YEAH, WELL... I'M GOING FOR A RECORD. DON'T TELL ANYBODY.
AT LEAST TELL ME YOU'RE TAKING YOUR THREE-DAY MEDICAL LEAVE.
I AM... BUT I'VE GOT TO FINISH UP SOMETHING IMPORTANT BEFORE I GO.
SURE IT WON'T WAIT UNTIL YOU GET BACK?

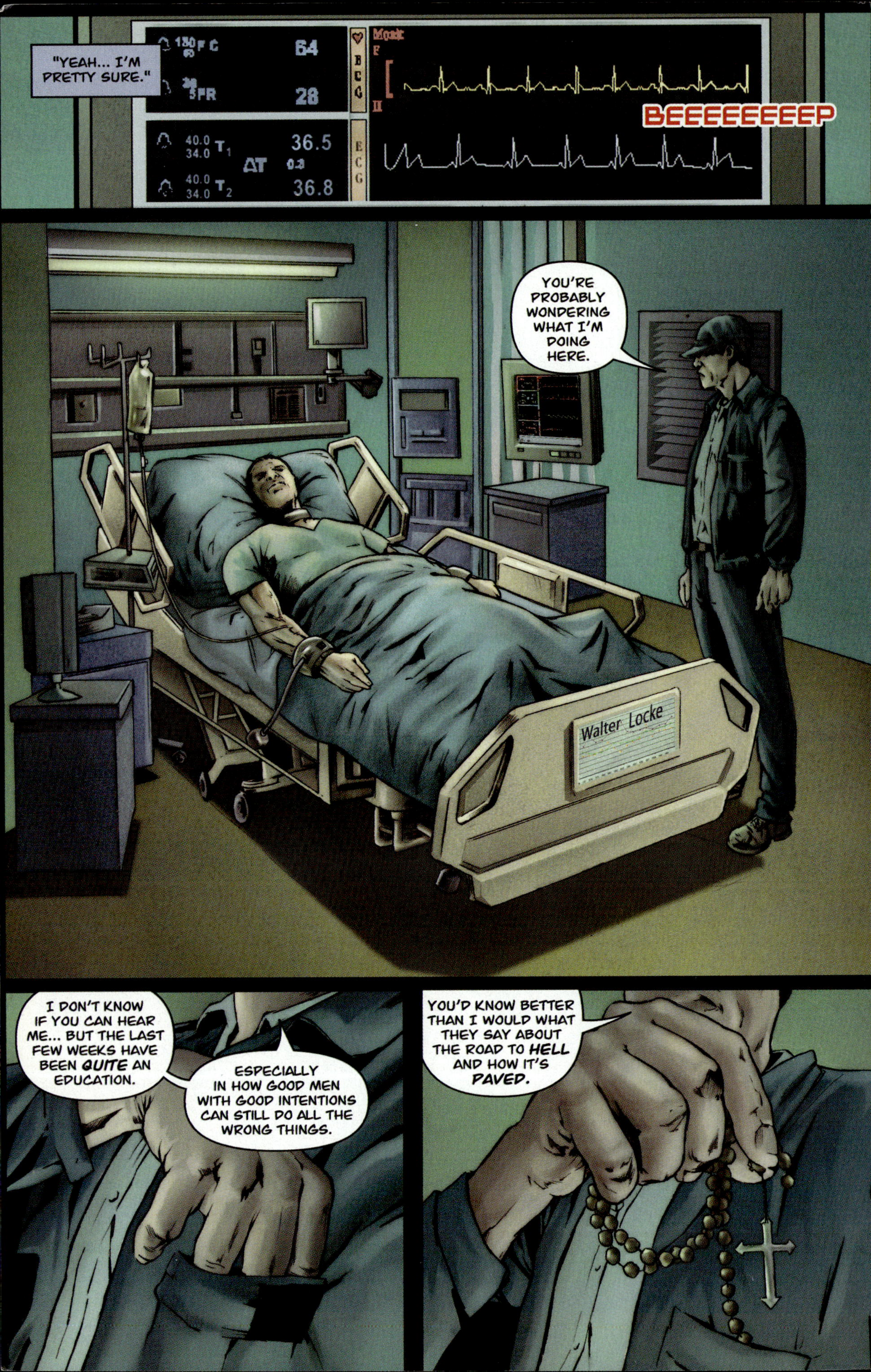

"YEAH... I'M PRETTY SURE."

BEEEEEEEEP

YOU'RE PROBABLY WONDERING WHAT I'M DOING HERE.

Walter Locke

WHAT I'M SAYING IS... I SHOULDN'T HAVE DONE TO YOU WHAT I DID. I SHOULD HAVE HAD A STRONGER WILL. I SHOULD HAVE FOUND A BETTER WAY.
AND I CAN'T TAKE THAT BACK.
YOU WERE A MURDERER, BUT YOU WERE ALSO A MAN OF GOD. AND YOU DESERVED BETTER.
FOR WHAT IT'S WORTH... I'M SORRY. I HOPE ONE DAY YOU CAN FORGIVE ME.

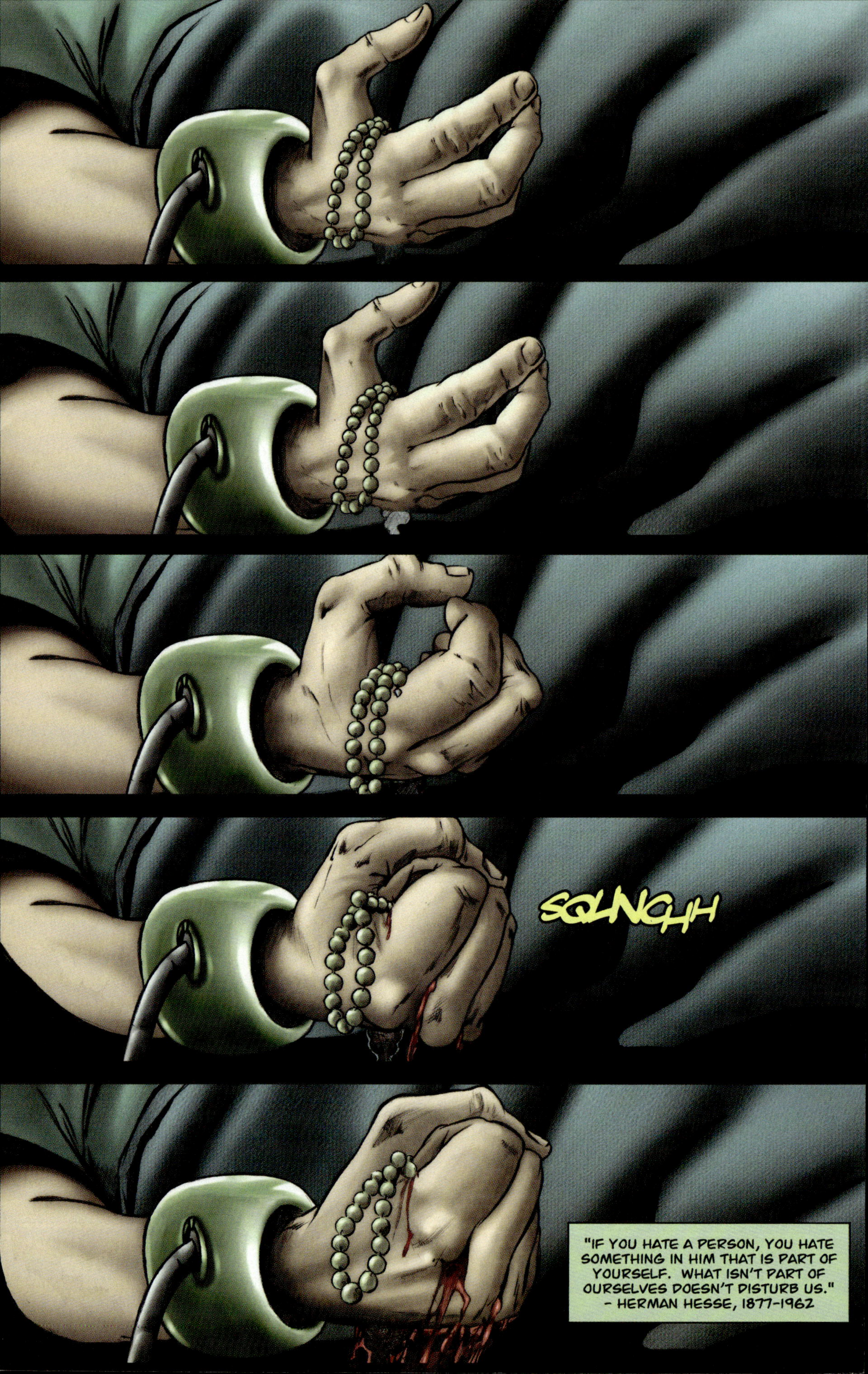
SQLNCHH
"IF YOU HATE A PERSON, YOU HATE SOMETHING IN HIM THAT IS PART OF YOURSELF. WHAT ISN'T PART OF OURSELVES DOESN'T DISTURB US."
- HERMAN HESSE, 1877-1962

CORRECTIVE
MEASURES

OVER DISSECTING A COVER

TING A COVER DISS

CORRECTIVE MEASURES

COVER DISSECTING A COVER

DISSECTING A COVER DIS

AXEL